Dog Romanc

Three Short Romance S

(Lucky Dog Series Collection)

Authored by Ava Summers

Personal
Plan Builder?
Premier
Food Intolerance
Testing

Remedy kitchen

Gainz kitchen
prep by gainz

Real meal

Batch & thyme

Love Yourself

Out of the box

Wild at heart

Premier meal prep

Root kitchen

Blueberry Hills ✓

Please consider leaving a review wherever you bought the book, or telling your friends about it, to help spread the word.

Table of Contents

Love Me, Love My Dog

Chapter 1

John entered the room.

"Hello, Anne. I expected to find you here." He walked toward her in his usual confident manner and...

"Damn it!" Samantha muttered. It was her second try at writing the final scene of her new romance novel. It seemed she wouldn't be able to finish it on time.

She started pacing around her writing room. There had to be something to help her get back into the groove.

Samantha rose up from the chair and walked into the kitchen to drink some water. The water rarely helped, but it didn't hurt to try. Besides, sitting in front of her laptop in front of an empty screen always made her thirsty. When you can't squeeze any words out of yourself, every reason is good enough to leave your work.

She poured water from a glass pitcher into a coffee mug and gulped it down. The silence in the house was overpowering. Back in L.A., there was always some kind of noise. Here, everything was quiet and sleepy. Too quiet.

It was the loneliness. That's why she couldn't write. The house was too quiet and empty. She just sat there all day long with little else to do. Something or someone to occupy her mind would help her write. Perhaps it was time to break out of her shell and make some friends in the town. Socializing had always been a struggle for her.

She looked out the window. An older woman walked her beagle down the street. The dog trotted right beside her with a happy expression on its face.

What if she made a different type of a friend? Samantha rushed back to her writing room. It was a bare-bones yellow-painted space with a single cheap folding brown desk in the back of the room and her laptop on top of it. She was far from living like a monk, but her writing room had to be minimalistic.

She sat at the desk and typed into the search engine, "Animal shelter Maple Hills." There was an animal shelter in the town. Samantha exhaled a long breath and clicked on the first result.

Pictures of dogs, cats, and rabbits appeared on her screen. The next cuter than the last, they all begged with their eyes to take them home and give them love they hadn't had the opportunity to experience.

The pictures of puppies and kittens from animal shelters always broke her heart. This time, Samantha wouldn't just look at the pictures. She was going to adopt a puppy. Robert wasn't around to tell her how much dogs stink. It was at least one perk of her divorce.

She noted down the address of the shelter and checked it on Google Maps. The shelter was at the end of the town, close to the horse riding school.

Samantha put on her white sneakers and grabbed the car keys lying on top of the granite countertop in the kitchen. She stomped out of her house and hopped into her car.

Chapter 2

The animal shelter in Maple Hills was an unconventional place.

The owners of the shelter, James and Melinda Brooke, had a true passion for their job.

The area that belonged to the shelter looked more like a residential home than an animal rescue. The office, a one-room building with stocked shelves of animal food, looked like a wooden cabin in the middle of Alaska. The small office building was surrounded by several tiny houses hosting the animals.

"We opened the shelter to give them a second chance, but not at the expense of making them feel like hell when waiting for a new owner. Hence the houses," Melinda said to Samantha when Samantha introduced herself to the couple and asked them why there were no cages.

Now Melinda was gone to tend to the rabbits, while James gave Samantha a tour of the shelter.

"Let's go this way," he said. James was a lanky 50-something brunet with gray strands of hair. He wore a white wool jumper, faded jeans and a pair of leather work gloves.

James led Samantha to a tiny wooden building across the office. They entered a spacious room with felt dog furniture. A pack of puppies slept at the back of the room in a brown-colored plush dog bed. The room smelled of hay that covered the floor.

"Here we have five beagle puppies from Jake Miller. If you're looking for a faithful companion, a beagle will be the right choice. Don't expect him to be a guard dog, though. Everyone can win over a beagle with some food."

"They're too cute." Samantha squatted near the puppies to pet them. One of the dogs opened its eyes and licked her hand.

"I gotta warn you, though. Beagles are easily bored. If you want to adopt one, I hope you can spend a lot of time with it."

"I work at home. I have plenty of free time."

"Good. We don't let everyone adopt our dogs. They need proper attention."

"That's understandable."

Another puppy woke up and yawned.

"Would you like to see our other puppies? We have some crossbreeds in another kennel right beside this one."

"Yes, please."

James led her to a tiny house standing next to the one they had just visited. The room was divided in two by a wooden wall with a door in the middle of it.

"Samantha, meet Apollo."

A cross between a schnauzer and poodle wagged its tail between her legs. It made circles around her and jumped at her legs.

"What's up with the door?" Samantha asked. She crouched down to pet the dog.

"Some dogs don't like each other. We don't have enough space to keep every dog in a different house, so we built the wall. We don't like fences."

Samantha liked the couple more and more. Who would have gone to such lengths to make animals feel at home rather than like in a prison? The only animal shelter Samantha visited in her life was the complete opposite of this place.

She could grow to love this small town. Nobody in L.A. would care that much about stray animals.

"Let's see how Prince is doing," James said. He opened the door in the wall and motioned her to get in.

Samantha couldn't name the breed of the dog. It reminded her of a friendly dog of her friend back in L.A. It was small, white and with long hair that covered its eyes.

Prince was anything but friendly. When he saw them enter the room, he started barking so loudly that she couldn't hear what James was saying.

"So young and so moody. We better leave him alone today. Melinda will come later to give him food," James said. He closed the door to Prince's room.

"Let me show you the other dogs. I'd like you to see all of them before you make a decision."

James led her to two other houses and showed her even more puppies, all of them as cute as the ones in the other kennels.

"It was the last one," James said. He closed the door to the kennel where he showed Samantha a dog that reminded her of a German shepherd, but James explained it was a crossbreed.

"How am I supposed to pick just one? They're all so cute it hurts," Samantha asked.

"How about you go home and sleep on it? I don't want you to make a hasty decision," he said.

Melinda left the office building and approached them. "Oh, hey, Melinda," James said.

Melinda Brooke was a mirror image of James. Tall and skinny, and wearing a similar pair of leather work gloves as James, she appeared like his sister, not his wife.

"Hey, Melinda, maybe you can help me out. How am I supposed to pick just one puppy out of all these sweet dogs?" Samantha asked.

"You could start with telling us how big of a dog you want. A beagle and a German shepherd won't be exactly of the same size when they grow."

"Frankly speaking, I haven't thought about it. I have a spacious place. It doesn't really matter if the dog is big."

A loud bark besides the office building interrupted their conversation. Something big was running in their direction.

"What's that?" Samantha asked.

"Oh, it's Winston. We let him wander outside during the day. He's too big for his kennel," James said. "Nobody wants him because everyone wants a puppy. Besides, he frightens people," Melinda said.

Before Samantha could ask why Winston frightened people, the biggest dog Samantha had ever seen emerged from behind the office and ran straight across them. She wanted to curl up on the ground and hope it wouldn't kill her.

Winston came to a halt a few feet away from her and trotted over to Melinda. Samantha felt as if her heart was going to beat out of her chest.

If James and Melinda weren't so tall, Winston, a gray, long-haired dog would probably be half their height. Samantha was five feet four, so when the dog approached her, its grey head was right above her hip bone. His head had to be twice as big as hers.

"Good boy," Melinda said and patted his huge head. The dog couldn't look happier. His brown eyes were so lit up they were almost orange.

"What breed is that? I have never seen such a big dog."

"I saw your frightened face. You thought you would die, didn't you?" Melinda chuckled.

"It's the Irish Wolfhound," James said. "The tallest dog in the world."

"How tall is he?"

"Thirty five inches, one hundred fifty pounds," James replied.

"Oh my God."

"The best part is when he stands on his hind legs. He's easily seven feet tall this way," Melinda said.

"How old is he exactly?" Samantha asked. The dog looked at her with an incredulous stare. She avoided eye contact with it in fear she would aggravate it.

"We don't know exactly, but he can't be older than three years. It's still too old for most people, though," Melinda replied.

"Besides, most people who come to us want a family dog, and they judge Winston by his looks. Actually, Irish Wolfhounds are tempered, patient and gentle. But try to tell them about it when they think they're on the brink of death," James said.

"How did he get here?" Samantha asked.

"One day, when I was tending to the horses in the evening, he appeared out of the blue. Got me thinking it was a rabid wild dog, but then he simply lay on the floor and looked at me as if asking for food," James said. "So I went to the pantry, got a bone with some meat on it and gave it to him. Been here ever since. He's the nicest dog ever."

Samantha looked at the dog with a mix of fear and admiration. It was scary, yet its eyes were calm, with no hint of aggression.

The dog sat in front of her and looked at her as if waiting for her to pet it.

"Okay, okay," Samantha said. She extended her hand to pet the dog. It opened its mouth and licked her fingers with a tongue that had to be longer than her hand.

"Yuck. We've only met each other and you're already exchanging your fluids with me?"

There was something in the dog that drew her to him. Perhaps it was the look in his eyes, confident yet thoughtful. Or maybe it was the way he was treated by people that reminded her of herself. They like them younger, don't they? Just like Robert and his doll back in California.

She was surprised she was so afraid of the dog in the beginning. Now that she was petting him, she knew he was anything but aggressive. She had never seen a dog that looked more peaceful than Winston.

"Gentle when stroked, fierce when provoked. That's what people say about them," James said, as if reading her mind.

Samantha couldn't imagine Winston angry. He wagged his tail in a circular motion and begged her to keep stroking his back.

"I want to adopt him. He's perfect."

"Are you sure? Don't you want to sleep on it?" James asked. He had a startled expression on his face. Samantha guessed people didn't adopt animals on their first visit.

"No. I made up my mind."

"What do you think, Melinda?" James said.

"Let the gal take him. I recognize love at first sight when I see it. Even when it starts with a near-death experience."

"So be it, then," he said.

James led Samantha to the office and asked her to fill out papers stating that she was adopting the dog. When she was done, Melinda came back with Winston on the leash and handed the leash to Samantha.

"Winston, behave yourself. Don't make us look bad in Samantha's eyes," Melinda said. Samantha noticed a tear forming in Melinda's eye.

"Oh, and if you ever need to go see a vet, call Chris Green. He's been our local veterinarian for quite a few years," James said. He pulled a white business card from his pocket and handed it to Samantha.

And just like that, Winston was now her dog.

Chapter 3

"Hey buddy, what's wrong?" Samantha asked. Her Irish Wolfhound lay with a sad look on its face near her work desk.

Winston has been with her for a few weeks already, and she had never seen him acting so sad.

When Winston vomited for the second time that morning, Samantha decided to take him to the veterinary clinic. She pulled out from the drawer the business card James handed her a couple weeks ago. She dialed the number, waited for a few rings, and hung up.

"Well, it won't hurt us to drive there and at least check the opening hours. Right, Winston?"

The dog just looked at her with no emotion instead of jumping at her as he always did when they were going somewhere by car.

"Okay, get up and let's go, boy."

Ten minutes later, Samantha pulled her car in front of a small beige-colored building with a big sign that said, "Maple Hills Veterinary Clinic."

She got out the car, opened the door on the passenger's side and motioned Winston to get out. He jumped out of the car with reluctance. It pained her to see him in such a condition.

The clinic was open, but the door to the main office was closed. Samantha could hear voices coming from the office, so she sat down in the chair and ordered Winston to lie beside her.

The waiting room was a small rectangular-shaped room with beige tiles and white walls. The whole place reminded her of a regular doctor's office, if it wasn't for the posters of animals on the walls and a bowl of water in the corner of the room.

"I'd like to check up on her in two days." Samantha heard a deep male voice right beside the door.

"Of course. See you on Thursday, then. Thank you, Chris," a female voice said.

A short brunette carrying a small ginger cat left the office. She glanced at Winston and left the room in a hurry. A tall thirty-something brunet with short hair and a full beard appeared in the doorstep of the office. He had a kind and warm face. His lively emerald eyes wandered toward Winston.

"Hello. I'm Chris Green." He extended his hand.

"Samantha Anderson." They shook hands.

"Samantha and...?"

"Winston."

"How can I help you today?"

"Winston has been behaving in a strange way recently. He's just lying in the house and doesn't want to go out. He didn't even touch his food today."

Winston vomited on the clean tiles as if to confirm what she has just said. "Oh, and it's the third time he vomited today. I'm sorry for that."

"No worries, I'll clean it later. Let me look at him in the office. Please come inside." He motioned them to get in.

Chris lowered the metal examination table to the floor and guided Winston to stand on it.

"Please sit down while I check him." He pulled the lever to raise the table.

While Chris examined Winston, Samantha took a moment to look at the room.

A white wooden desk in front of her had a stack of papers on it. She saw a desk calendar with a picture of a St. Bernard, a plain brown organizer, and a couple of pens.

At her left, behind the examination table, was a white rack with a shelf of neatly stacked small bottles and a box of disposable white gloves Chris pulled on his hands before examining Winston. It was an office of a person who had liked order.

Samantha looked with concern at Winston standing on the table with his head bowed.

"Does he have diarrhea?" Chris asked.

"I'm not sure. When I take him for a walk, I don't keep him on a leash."

"His symptoms indicate it's food poisoning. Fortunately, it's nothing serious. I can give him some medicine to ease the pain."

"Oh, thank God it's nothing serious. I was getting worried."

"Don't worry. He probably just ate something spoiled. He should feel much better in just a day or two. Let me write you a prescription."

When Chris was busy writing the prescription, Samantha examined his face.

His greenish-blue eyes were of almost the same color as his scrubs. His short brown beard was neatly trimmed. She didn't like beards in men, but she had to admit it fitted him.

Samantha's eyes slipped down to his wide forearms. They reminded her of the forearms of a tennis player.

"Please give it to him two times today. If he's still vomiting tomorrow, give him another one." Chris raised his head and startled her with sudden strong eye contact.

When he handed her the prescription, their fingers touched for a second. The gentle pressure sent a small shiver up her spine. Samantha felt something she didn't expect to feel toward a random stranger a couple minutes after meeting him.

Samantha looked at the prescription with uncertainty.

"The pharmacy is just around the corner. You're new here, aren't you?"

"I moved here a few weeks ago. How did you know?"

"The look on your face. Besides, I have never seen you before. I recognize all people from the town, even if I don't know their names."

Samantha was glad he misunderstood her confusion. She knew where the pharmacy was. What she didn't know was why he threw her off balance. She had a passing thought of getting to know him a bit better, more than just as a neighbor. She scolded herself for her unusual thoughts.

"Well, I think I must get… get going."

"If Winston doesn't get better by Thursday, please come again."

"Thank you. I hope it won't be necessary. Winston, let's go." She guided her dog out of the office. She hoped Chris hadn't noticed her wobbly legs.

Chapter 4

"Winston, where are you?"

Samantha had been so lost in writing her newest novel that she didn't notice her dog was no longer snoring beside her working desk.

She already checked the kitchen, the bedroom, and the guest room. She didn't remember leaving any doors open, but now she wasn't sure about it. She ventured outside.

"Winston!"

The dog was nowhere in sight. He must have somehow escaped. She shouted for him once again. The singing of the birds was the only reply.

Samantha inspected the brown wooden fence to find any possible place Winston could escape. The fence was high enough that he couldn't jump over it, so the only possible way had to be either under it or through the gate. She heard a movement beside the fence.

"Winston?"

A squirrel appeared on a tree branch right beside the fence. Her house shared the eastern part with a thick forest. She was terrified that the dog got lost in the woods. She ventured back to her house and grabbed car keys.

When she was about to drive away, she saw Winston walking down the street with a happy look on his face right beside a St. Bernard kept on a leash by Chris. She got out of the car and approached them standing near the gate.

"What is going on?" Samantha asked.

"Your crazy dog appeared out of nowhere in the forest when I was taking a walk with Elsa. I thought it was a large wolf until he came closer. Then I remembered your visit last week."

A broad smile illuminated his face. He looked completely different than the professional veterinarian she met a week ago. His casual clothing made him look even more attractive than his professional attire.

“I have no idea how it happened. One moment he was right beside me, a second later he was gone.”

“Thankfully he had his tag on. If I didn’t know where you lived, I would probably take him to the Brookes’.”

Samantha wanted to go home as soon as possible. Chris made her feel like a shy teenager, and she didn’t like this feeling at all. She was too old for that.

“Thank you for walking him home. I appreciate it. Winston, heel!”

But Winston wouldn’t budge. He was busy playing with Elsa and heeded no attention to Samantha’s order.

“Winston!”

“I think he wants to play with Elsa a little longer. Why don’t you take him for a walk with us? You’ll most certainly make Winston happy.”

Winston stopped playing with Elsa and looked at Samantha with begging eyes. What the heck, did he learn how to read minds?

Samantha was glad she didn’t have any children. She couldn’t handle the begging eyes of her dog, let alone the begging eyes of a kid.

“I… Why not.” She looked at Winston with feigned anger. “Let me grab his leash. I’ll be back in a second.”

Samantha trotted over to the house and entered the bathroom. She combed her brown hair and rushed out of the bathroom. There was no time to make herself prettier. She went to kitchen and grabbed Winston’s leash from a hook.

When she went outside, Chris was busy throwing the dogs Frisbee. Samantha bought it for Winston a couple days ago to give him more exercise in the backyard in addition to their regular walks.

She descended the steps of the porch and joined them.

“I’m ready,” she said. They walked together to the forest where they let their dogs loose to play. The dogs started chasing after each other, running in circles and jumping. They were an imposing couple – two dogs that were almost taller than her three year old niece Angela.

“You didn’t come again last week, so I guess Winston got better.”

“He was back to his usual self two days later. Thank you again for your help.”

“That’s my job. I’m glad I could help. You were lucky to catch me at noon last week. I usually don’t open before two o’clock.”

They walked for a minute in silence.

“So, what brought you to Maple Hills?” Chris asked.

“Escape. The new beginning. I wanted to get away from the city.” She scolded herself for sharing too much information with him.

“You’ve definitely came to the right place. There are few places quieter than Maple Hills, unless you like the farm living.” It seemed the broad smile rarely left his face. God, he was so handsome when he smiled like this.

Chris was so calm and easygoing. Everything about him was peaceful. She liked his simple outfit – raw denim jeans and a tailored blue shirt with rolled cuffs that exposed his muscular forearms.

“What about you? How long have you been living here?” she asked.

“I was born here. Left the town to go to the veterinary college and intern. Couldn’t wait to get back here to open my own clinic.”

Winston kept chasing after Elsa as if they were the best of friends. He usually appeared thoughtful to Samantha, but now he just looked foolish.

"Do you work in the town?" Chris asked.

"I work at home. I write books." She dreaded his next question.

"What kind of books?"

"Um... Romance novels."

God, he made her feel so nervous, and now he was asking questions about her books. Samantha sometimes blushed talking about her books with her family, let alone with a stranger.

"That's interesting. I have never met a writer in my life. I would love to read one of your books. I love any kind of good fiction."

"I... Of course, I have some of my old books in the attic."

"Great, I'll take you up on that offer."

Samantha regretted telling him about the books.

They kept following a dirt trail in the middle of the pine forest. For a minute, neither of them said a word.

The dogs put an end to the awkward silence. Winston appeared with Elsa carrying a big stick in her mouth. Chris took it from her and threw it in front of them. Both dogs started running at the same time, as if they were competing in the Olympics.

"Let me take you to my secret place," Chris said. He briefly touched her lower back to guide her to a small trail between the trees.

His touch sent a shiver down her spine. Why was she acting like a teenager? He was handsome, but so what. She was done with men after what Robert had done to her.

They followed the trail for a minute or so when a small opening appeared in front of them. A small wooden bench stood right beside a forest stream surrounded by moss-covered stones. Chirping of the birds accompanied the relaxing sound of the running water.

"Wow, it's so beautiful," she said.

"Let's sit here for a while." Chris motioned her to the bench situated beside the stream. "I come here to recharge my batteries after work. Nothing is better than solitude in nature."

Samantha sat down at the edge of the bench. She didn't want to sit so close to him. His calm confidence intimidated her.

"How do you like the town? Does it help you write your novels?"

"At first it was too quiet for me. It all changed when I adopted Winston."

"Did you get him from the Brookes?"

"I did. I wanted a puppy, but when Winston showed up, I felt as if he was waiting for me."

Samantha smiled, thinking about the first days with Winston at home.

"I could see how you looked at him at the clinic. There are people who love their dogs, and there are people who adore them."

"Why a veterinarian?"

"I have always loved animals. It's in my genes, I guess. My grandfather was a dog breeder."

"What about your parents? Do they love animals, too?"

"They passed away three years ago."

"I'm sorry."

Chris threw a small rock into the stream.

"Elsa was their dog. Just a puppy when they died," he said. "Let's get going. I have a surgery at four. Auntie Florence would be pissed off if I was late," he said.

They took the same route back. Their dogs were still chasing after each other as if they could never tire out.

"Your aunt lives in the town?" she asked.

"She's been living here her entire life."

"What's wrong with her dog?"

"Nothing. He just needs to be neutered. He's impossible when chasing ladies."

When they reached the edge of the forest, they took their dogs on the leash. Samantha and Chris stood at the beginning of the trail and looked at each other. Their pets were finally tired of playing with each other and just sat down, watching the surroundings.

"I enjoyed talking with you. Why don't we grab some coffee sometime this week?" Chris asked.

Her cold mind said no, her emotions said yes.

"Why not," she said, trying to sound casual. They exchanged phone numbers. When she was giving him her number, she glanced at his fingers. She was surprised there was no wedding band on his hand. He had to be at least thirty five. A divorcee, then, just like her. Or perhaps a widower.

"I'll call you at the end of this week. Is that okay?" he said.

"Sure."

He surprised Samantha by hugging her. It was just a casual gesture, but it still got her heart beating faster. She wondered if he hugged every stranger like that.

"See you. Oh, and sorry for Winston. I didn't want him to interrupt your walk. I still have no idea how he got out."

"No worries. If it wasn't for him, we wouldn't have met today. And *that* would have been a pity."

Chapter 5

"And then he told me how *that* would have been a pity if we haven't met. Can you believe it, Sarah?"

"He sounds like a nice guy, girl. Why don't you just let your guard down and enjoy it?"

Samantha always envied her younger sister's deep, warm voice. But then again, as an actress, she had her share of vocal exercises.

"I don't know. I feel he's just nice because I'm new in town."

"After the whole situation with Robert you deserve someone more worthy of you. Maybe he's the one?"

"Oh, Sarah, stop it. He's at least ten years younger than me."

"Why do you talk about him with so much passion, then?"

"I already told you. It's just nice to make friends in a new place."

"Right."

"Okay, okay. I give up. I think he's handsome. There, satisfied?"

"Nope. Tell me more about him."

"He seems like a carefree type. He always has this kind warm smile on his face."

"What does he look like?"

"He has short brown hair and a beard."

"A beard? Seriously? A guy with a beard is attractive to you?"

"I know, I know. But it fits him. Makes him look a little rugged. In a good way."

"There has to be something really special about him."

"I just like the way he makes me feel around him. Makes me feel welcomed here."

"I'm glad to hear that, sister. You can't keep living like a nun."

"Sarah, I'm forty-three. He's maybe thirty-five. If anything, we will become friends, nothing more."

"Friends? Please. Listen to yourself, girl. Talking like an old woman. Do you want me to send you a knitting kit?"

"Sarah…"

"But seriously, Samantha, you're an attractive, mature woman. You're caring, intelligent and straight up sexy."

"Tell it to Robert."

"Forget about this asshole. Move on."

"Easier said than done."

"You have the perfect opportunity now. Show Chris all you've got, Sam.""Thank you, Sarah. I'll think about it."

"Don't think about it. Do it. Anyway, I need to go. Take care, girl. Have fun with Mr. Vet."

Samantha hung up and turned her attention to Winston. The dog lay near the couch in the living room. He raised his head and gazed at her as if he knew she had been looking at him.

"Look what you did. You couldn't just stay inside, could you?"

Winston stared at her with a twinkle in his eye, almost as if he was thinking, "The joke's on you."

His intelligence sometimes frightened Samantha. It felt as if there was a real human being hidden underneath the dog's fur.

Samantha went to her writing room to finish the last chapter of her new novel. As usual, Winston accompanied her and sat down beside the desk.

"Is there anything else you want to tell me?"

The dog tilted his head to one side as if he didn't know what she was talking about.

But Samantha knew he was just playing with her. There was something mischievous in his brown eyes.

Chapter 6

"Winston, stop!" Samantha yelled.

The dog chased away after a squirrel into the deep forest. She stood on a dirt trail surrounded by towering pine and birch trees. She has never been so deep in the forest. She was scared Winston wouldn't find his way back.

"Winston!" she yelled again.

Samantha stood on the trail and looked around in all directions. She didn't hear any sound except for the chirping of the birds and wind rustling through the leaves.

She entered the thick forest where Winston had disappeared a few minutes ago. One of the benefits of having a huge dog was that he left visible tracks. Even an amateur could track him. Or so she thought.

Samantha followed the trail her dog took through the forest. Two minutes later, she realized she got lost. The forest was much darker than on the trail and she could no longer make out the tracks. Samantha felt as if the woods had been swallowing her. There were trees and shrubs all around her. She shuddered. Without Winston beside her, the forest felt threatening.

She dug in her pocket and pulled out her cell phone. No reception. Perfect. She went on a longer walk to get her thoughts together. Now she just added another thing to worry about. First, how to find Winston. Second, how to get back to town.

She turned around and took a path she thought would lead her back to the trail. Loud barking echoed through the forest. It was Winston. Samantha yelled for him.

She heard heavy steps of something big running through the forest. Winston wasn't alone. Either something chased him or the dog found a companion. Samantha hoped it was the latter.

The noise became louder and louder. She strained her eyes and noticed Winston's fur between the pine trees in front of her. A dog with white and brown spots ran beside him. The noise the dogs made together had been so loud that everything that lived nearby was probably scared out of its skin.

Samantha came to a small opening and saw Winston and Elsa emerging from the shrubs across from her. The feeling of relief was replaced with embarrassment. Where there was Elsa, there had to be Chris. Perfect.

Winston trotted over her and barked as if to say, "Follow me." Elsa looked at them from distance. It was obvious she was waiting for her master.

Samantha followed Winston and Elsa through the forest. They led her over a small hill. The trail was right on the other side. She climbed it down. Chris stood on the trail and looked startled at her.

"Samantha? What are you doing here?"

"I… I was looking for mushrooms."

"Mushrooms?"

"Okay, you caught me. I got lost. Winston chased after a squirrel and I followed him into the woods."

Chris laughed. "You're not the first person who got lost here. There's nothing to be embarrassed about. You okay?"

"I'm fine." She was glad she wore long pants. If she had shorts, her legs would have small cuts just like her arms. She was so stupid to enter the forest instead of following the trail back home.

"We should clean your cuts, just to be sure."

"Did you hear me? I said I'm fine."

Samantha immediately felt guilty for yelling at Chris. It was only her stupidity that she got lost in the forest.

"I'm sorry, Chris. I didn't mean to yell at you."

"No worries. Let's head back to town."

They followed the narrow trail through the forest. Samantha walked behind Chris, while their dogs led the way.

A few minutes later they emerged from the forest on the other side of the town. Samantha realized she hadn't been that deep in the forest after all. They were just one block away from the veterinary clinic. She had circled around the town while she had been in the forest.

They leashed their dogs and walked down the street.

"Are you sure you don't want to get these cuts cleaned? It won't take longer than two minutes. I live just around the corner," Chris said.

"Okay. You're the doctor here."

Chris led her to his house. He lived just two blocks away from the clinic in a small one-story house with a quaint front porch and an old-fashioned flower box. He pulled out the keys from his pocket and opened the door.

"You stay here and play," he said to the dogs.

Samantha and Chris walked inside. His house was just like his clinic – orderly and extremely clean. She liked the simple design of his house. The small hallway had cream tiles and an old wooden shoe cabinet. She was surprised to see a glass vase with big yellow flowers on it. It added an old-fashioned feel to the room. Chris led her to the living room.

"Please make yourself comfortable. I'll be back in a second."

Samantha sat down on the sofa in the middle of the room. At her left stood two brown wooden bookshelves that covered the entire wall. In the corner of the room, right beside the bookshelves, stood a rocking chair. There was a small table on the other side of the room. She saw a drawing paper and a couple of pencils on it.

Samantha walked to the table and looked at the paper. It was an unfinished drawing of a forty-something woman with an oval face, long dark hair, almond-shaped eyes and full lips. A feeling of joy spread throughout her body when she realized it was her portrait. He wouldn't draw her if she was just a random stranger to him, would he?

She heard approaching footsteps and returned to the sofa. Chris entered the room with a small bowl of water and cotton pads.

"Please give me your hand."

She put her right hand palm up on his lap. He dipped a cotton pad in water and started cleaning her cuts. It burned, but she didn't want to act weak in front of him.

"There you go. Please give me the left hand."

Chris cleaned her left hand. She was almost glad she had gotten lost in the forest. His gentle touch felt like a sensual massage. And the drawing. Chris drew her portrait. That knowledge alone more than made up for the fear and embarrassment of getting lost in the woods.

"Why no hydrogen peroxide?" she asked.

"It's ineffective as a disinfectant. It can even slow healing and lead to scarring."

"Seriously?"

"I'm the doctor here. Remember?"

"Right, I'm sorry, Doc."

He beamed at her. She liked how lively his eyes became when he smiled. He looked as if he had no care in the world.

"By the way, how about coffee tomorrow? I wanted to call you in the evening, but since we've already met, I guess we can talk about it now," Chris said.

"Tomorrow is fine. When would you like to meet?"

"Noon? I open my clinic at two o'clock."

"Noon works for me."

"Perfect. I'll take you to the best café in the town. I guarantee you have never had better coffee."

"I'm looking forward to it." She rose from the sofa. "Well, I better get going. I don't want to take up any more of your time."

"It's okay. It's not even noon. I still have two hours before I need to open the clinic."

The sound of his cell phone interrupted their conversation.

"Hi, Katie. How can I help you?" Chris said. "Of course. No problem. Please come. I'll be there in twenty minutes."

He hung up the phone and looked at Samantha.

"Well, it seems our time is indeed over. I need to go to the clinic now."

"It's okay, I was just leaving."

Chris walked her to the front door.

"See you tomorrow. I'll pick you up at noon."

"See you. And thanks for taking care of the cuts."

"The pleasure is all mine."

He gave her a hug. Samantha could've sworn it was much longer than their first hug.

Chapter 7

Samantha was looking at herself in the mirror for the third time.

She wore a knee-length red summer dress and strappy silver heels. She made beach waves in her auburn hair – one of her favorite styles because it was always super easy to create. Besides, Sarah told her she looked stunning with simple hairstyles.

She grabbed her purse and was about to look at herself in the mirror for the fourth time when the doorbell rang.

"Hi there," Chris said. She felt herself blushing when he gazed at her with awe.

He wore a dark grey jacket, light blue shirt, navy pants and a pair of brown wingtips – certainly not his regular everyday outfit. She was glad she didn't go with a pair of comfortable jeans and a regular shirt, something she considered before talking about it with her sister.

"Hello." Samantha felt shaky in his presence. He looked so handsome in his jacket and blue shirt.

"Are we going to keep talking at the doorstep?" Chris asked amused.

"No, of course not, let's go."

When she was about to leave the house, Winston appeared out of the kitchen and ran toward Chris as if he were his best friend he hadn't seen for years.

"Hey buddy," Chris said and patted the happy dog on the head.

"See you later, Winston. Behave yourself," she said and closed the door.

When they arrived at the café with a huge "Black Bean Café" sign over it, Samantha was surprised to see it was so full. People sat at the small brown wooden tables and on two sofas in the back of the room.

The interior of the café wouldn't win any design awards, but there was nothing to complain about, either. The tables were simple, but didn't look cheap. The light brown walls were decorated with illustrations and drawings of various places from the town. Samantha recognized the illustration of the town hall and the main street.

The central point of the café was a long wooden counter. Two twenty-something waiters stood behind it. On the counter stood a black board with specials written on it with white chalk.

Chris led her to a quiet table in the corner of the room. They ordered their coffee.

"Looks like a nice place," Samantha said.

"It's one of the best places here. But then again, it's a small town. It's not like you have a wide selection of locales."

"I like it here."

"I'm glad to hear that. Not all people can appreciate the slow pace of a small town. You moved here from L.A., right?

"How did you know?"

"Just a guess. I saw your registration plates."

The waiter brought their coffee.

Samantha took a sip of her coffee. "Oh my God, it's delicious."

"Told you it's the best coffee in the world." A triumphant smile lit up his face.

"Did you draw any of the drawings here?" she asked and pointed to the walls.

"How do you know that I draw?"

"I saw a drawing paper and pencils in your house."

Chris blushed. It seemed there had been something more to the portrait of her than just a habit of drawing every new stranger, after all.

"I… Yes, there are a couple of my drawings here. The one over there with the dog -- that's Elsa -- and the one right there depicting the main street. There's also my other drawing on the other side of the room. It shows my secret place."

"So it's not such a secret place, after all."

"It's not like I attached the map to the drawing. And it might as well be a product of my imagination."

"Right, I didn't think about it."

"What about you? Do you have any secret talents I should know about?"

"I have a talent of getting lost in the woods five minutes away from the town."

"That's impressive."

"It is. You should try it."

"Maybe someday."

"Jokes aside, how did Winston even find you?"

"Dogs have great smell. He must have somehow smelled Elsa."

"I forgot to thank you for helping me find my way back."

"It wasn't me. You should thank Winston. He ran to me and barked like a wild dog. At first I thought you would be right behind him, but when he didn't stop barking I knew something was up. That's why we found you."

A twenty-something busty blonde woman dressed in tight jeans and a white top approached their table. She stood beside Chris and put her hand on his shoulder.

"Hey, Chris, sweetheart."

"Hi, Victoria," Chris said. Samantha heard a hint of anger in his voice.

She took an immediate dislike to the woman. She didn't introduce herself, as if Samantha wasn't worth her attention. Disappointment crept up on Samantha's face. Chris had a girlfriend, after all. The portrait, the walks, their meeting at the café, it was just him being friendly with her.

"Do you have a minute?" Victoria asked.

"Not now, Vic. Can't you see I'm not alone?"

"Okay, okay, I'm sorry. Don't get mad at me, Chris. I'll call you later, then. Bye."

Chris didn't bother replying.

"Let's get going. It's already past one. I don't want to open late," he said to Samantha, as if leaving the place would erase from her head the strange meeting with Victoria.

They paid the bill and left the café. Chris drove her back home without saying a word. Whatever happened in the café between him and Victoria made him pretty rattled. When Samantha came back home, she couldn't find Winston anywhere in the house. She checked all the rooms in the house and the backyard. The dog was nowhere in sight.

When she was about to go looking for the dog in the forest, her phone rang. It was Chris.

"Hello?" she said.

"Winston is at my porch. Please come and take him."

"What the hell is this dog doing? I'll be there in a second."

Five minutes later, Samantha parked her car in front of Chris's house. Winston greeted her with Elsa, while Chris looked at her from the porch.

"Winston, what are you doing here?" she asked.

The dog looked at her and shifted his attention back to Elsa.

"I have no idea how he got here," she said to Chris, who stood at the steps of the porch.

"He knew his way here. As for how he got out of your house, I have no idea, either."

"I'm sorry, Chris. I'll find a way to keep him at home. I probably forgot to close all the windows."

"It's okay, forget about it. Listen Samantha, I saw the look on your face when Victoria approached us. I'll explain everything later."

"What do you want to explain, Chris? We've just met for coffee. You don't have to tell me about your girlfriend."

"It wasn't *just* coffee for me. And she isn't my girlfriend."

"She sure sounded like one. And the way you acted when she left us… Anyway, there's nothing to explain. We're just…"

Chris put two fingers on her lips and hushed her. His sensual touch lingered on her face even when he withdrew his hand.

"Listen, Samantha. I don't want to be just friends. I know you don't want it, either."

His boldness made her mad. He talked to her as if he knew everything about her.

"What do you know? I'm forty-three, for God's sake, and you're at least ten years younger. Do you really think I thought there would be something between us?"

Chris didn't reply. Instead, he touched her cheek with his soft fingers, brought her face to his and gave her a light, slow kiss. All her anger was gone in an instant.

She felt an intense desire to kiss him again and again and again. Oh God, how she missed kissing. Deep, passionate kissing. But she knew she couldn't just let herself go and be vulnerable again.

"Yes, that's what I thought. And you thought it, too," he said.

"I… I have to go. We'll talk later."

Samantha descended the steps, grabbed Winston by the collar and guided him to the car. Chris stood confused at the porch steps.

Chapter 8

"I don't know what to think. He kissed me, but this girl called him 'sweetheart,' Sarah."

"Take your time, girl. Sleep on it. Meet with him tomorrow and see what he says then. No need to worry."

"No need to worry. Why do you always have to be so upbeat and laid back?"

"Gotta be like that if you're an actress. Besides, you said he's into you. Why act so desperate, then?"

"What did I say?"

"You told me he drew your portrait."

"It doesn't mean he's into me."

"Right. And then when he told you he just doesn't want to be your friend, was that just a mistake on his part? A blunder? Oh, right. He wanted to say he wants to be your best friend, nothing more."

"Sarah..."

"Samantha, what do you really think about him? Can you be honest with me?"

"I don't know. It's driving me crazy. He made me nervous when I met him for the first time. I couldn't stop looking at his forearms and his smile."

"Oh, look, is Sam getting butterflies in her stomach?"

"Stop it, Sarah. You're crossing the line here."

"Sorry, girl. I didn't mean it this way. Seriously, go back to your novel, forget about Chris for a while and talk with him tomorrow. Talk it over. This Vivian or whatever her name was may have been just his friend."

"Victoria. And really, if you saw her, you would know why I'm so rattled now. The girl looked like straight out the model runway. Who am I compared to her?"

"You're a mature and attractive woman in her early forties. Life ain't over when you're forty, you know? He doesn't care about her if he kissed you."

"Yeah, right. Sarah, you're so naïve sometimes. Robert more than just kissed his blondie, and he was my husband at that time.."

"I know, girl. But let's not talk about it right now. You're still an attractive woman. I know you looked stunning in that red dress. I wish I saw the look in his eyes when he saw you."

The doorbell interrupted her conversation.

"I'm sorry Sarah, someone's at the door. I'll call you back later."

When she opened the door, she saw Victoria standing in the doorstep. She had a grim look on her face.

"What are you doing here?" Samantha asked.

"Just wanted to give you a word of caution. Chris is mine. Leave him alone, or I'll make your life miserable." Her words slashed the air like a sword.

"How did you know where to find me? And what do you want from me?"

"News travels fast in small towns. I bet they didn't teach you that in L.A., dinosaur. Stay away from Chris. He's mine."

"Leave my property, or I'll call the police."

"Don't worry. I was just leaving. Don't you ever kiss him again, or there will be consequences. Maybe something would happen to your beloved doggie?"

Winston appeared in the doorstep and growled at the woman, making her leave with a frightened face.

"Good job, Winston. You perfectly conveyed my emotions."

Samantha took Winston on a long walk to let off steam. When she came back, she listened to her sister's advice and went back to work on her novel. As a way to release her anger, she made Victoria one of the antagonists in her new romance.

A few hours later, her phone rang.

"Samantha, we need to talk. Can I come over?" Chris said.

"Okay."

"I'll be there in a jiffy."

Five minutes later, her doorbell rang. She didn't make the same mistake as before and checked who was standing at the doorstep before she opened the door. It was Chris.

"I'm sorry."

"What do you feel sorry for?" She motioned him to come in.

"For Victoria. I should have known she may see us there. It wasn't her shift, but she frequently hangs out at the café even after work."

Samantha led Chris to the living room. She sat on the couch, while Chris chose an armchair standing across her. Winston was nowhere to be seen. Samantha suspected he was in a deep sleep after a long and tiring walk.

"Who is she to you?"

"She's my ex-girlfriend. We had a… a short-term relationship. It was a couple years ago.

"So what is she doing in your life right now?"

"After our breakup, she has never stopped meddling in my personal life. I thought she was finally done with her temper tantrums."

"Well, that's a good way to put it. She was here today."

"What? Victoria was at your home today? Why?"

Samantha told Chris what Victoria had said to her.

"She went too far this time. This can't go on like that," he said.

"What should I do? I don't want anything bad happening to Winston."

Chris rose from the armchair and sat down on the couch right beside Samantha. He put a hand on her knee.

"Nothing will happen to Winston or you. She might be crazy, but she wouldn't hurt anybody," he said.

He put his muscular arms around Samantha. Their faces were so close to each other she could look deep into his jade eyes. Samantha saw the longing there. She wondered if he saw the anticipation in her eyes.

"Samantha, you are so beautiful," he said. He traced her cheek with his fingertips. She felt her skin prickle.

"Please kiss me," she whispered.

His soft lips touched hers. A warm feeling of excitement spread over her body, the kind of heat she felt for the last time more than a year ago.

"Please don't stop."

His gentle, yet passionate kissing made her lips engorged with blood. Chris kissed the nape of her neck. He moved from bare skin into her hair, and fluttered the tip of his tongue over her hair follicles. His tongue caressing her earlobe sent shivers down her back. A minute longer, and she wouldn't be able to resist him any longer.

"Chris, we should stop."

He withdrew his face. "It's okay. I don't want to rush it."

"I... I'm not ready yet. I... it's just too overwhelming. Too many things, too fast."

"It's okay. You don't have to explain anything."

"Chris, why me? What do you see in a forty-three year old woman?"

"What do I see in you? I see glowing chestnut hair, a kind and warm face, hazel eyes I can't stop staring at and lips that beg to be kissed. Samantha, you're a beautiful woman."

"I… Thank you." Nobody had ever described her in such a touching way.

"Tell you what… Why don't we take things slowly, get to know each other better. I have a dinner with my aunt tomorrow evening. I'd love you to come. She's a huge fan of your books."

His casual tone cleared the tension lingering in the air between them.

"Really? How do you know?"

"She told me her favorite romance writer moved here. I asked her who, and she said Samantha Anderson. I haven't heard about any other Samantha Anderson who has moved to Maple Hills recently."

"Caught red-handed." A smile appeared on her face. The way he joked with her put her at ease.

"So, what do you think? My aunt is a great cook. But she only cooks vegetarian food."

"I'm vegetarian, too. Have been one for five years already. My sister converted me."

"Well, then it's a good thing. You two will get along. I'll be here at seven tomorrow. Is that okay?"

"Sure. What should I bring?"

"You don't have to bring anything."

"But I want to. I don't want to go empty-handed."

"Why don't you bring one of your books? She would love to get a signed copy from you."

"I have a few copies of my new book somewhere around here. I can bring it with me. It's going to be in stores next week, so she hasn't read it yet."

"Sounds good. I'll see you tomorrow then. I don't want to keep you up late."

He rose from the couch. Samantha glanced at the watch and saw it was already eleven. Time flies fast when you're having fun.

She accompanied him to the door. Chris pulled her in a tight embrace, his chest pressed hard against her own. She wasn't sure if it was hers or his heart beating so fast, or perhaps they were both beating fast in unison.

He kissed her once again. His warm lips touched hers and tempted her to pull him by his shirt and make him stay for the night. She blushed, embarrassed by her naughty thoughts.

"Good night, Samantha."

"Good night, Chris."

He opened the door. She looked at him descending the steps of her porch. He turned around on his heels.

"One more thing…" he said.

"Yes?"

"Make it two. You promised me one of your books."

Chapter 9

"Oh, thank you dear. It's so nice of you," said Florence, Chris's aunt.

She was a short-haired, stout woman with maroon glasses that made her look like a fifty-something librarian. Her eyes lit up when Samantha introduced herself and gave Florence her signed newest book.

"Let's sit down and eat. I don't want you to eat my frittata cold." She motioned them to sit at the big square brown wooden dining table.

The cozy dining room reminded Samantha of her parent's house. They too liked brown shades of furniture and simple decorations on the walls.

A small beagle came out from under the table. It wagged its tail with joy and jumped on Samantha's legs.

"Hi there. What's your name?" she asked.

"It's Gus," Chris said.

Florence entered the room with a large round plate with something that looked like pizza. She put the plate on the table. If it wasn't for the vegetables cooked inside the frittata, it could pass for an extremely thick pizza. A delicious-looking one, at that.

"So, how did you get to know each other?" Florence asked. Samantha was sure Florence had already known it, but she played along. It was better to make some small talk than eat in awkward silence.

"My dog was sick. I had to take him to a vet."

"You couldn't have found a better veterinarian than my Chris. Isn't it right, Chris?"

"Oh, Auntie, stop it."

"How do you like the town, dear?"

"I love it here. It takes some time getting used to when you move from a big city, though."

"This place grows on you."

"Sure it does," Chris added.

"Mrs. Smith, your frittata is one of the most delicious things I've ever eaten."

"Thank you, dear. I'm glad to hear that."

"Auntie is probably the best cook in town."

"Chris..." Florence said.

"Are you a cook by profession?"

"No, I'm a high school teacher. I *was* a high school teacher," she smiled, as if thinking about the good old times. "I even taught Chris. Straight A's, this one."

"Biology?" Samantha guessed.

"You're one smart cookie, my dear."

When the dinner was over, Florence brought out a lemon cake. Samantha thought she was full when she had finished her plate. When she saw the beautiful white and yellow cake, her appetite was back with a vengeance.

The cake was even more delicious than the frittata.

When they finished the dessert, Samantha noticed it was already ten. She glanced at Chris and pointed at her watch.

"Auntie, we better get going. It's really late." Chris rose up from his chair.

"Thank you, Mrs. Smith. The food was absolutely delicious. It was a pleasure meeting you." She offered her hand.

"The pleasure is all mine, sweetheart, all mine." Florence shook Samantha's hand with the vigor of a young person. "And thank you for the book. A perfect gift for a lazy summer afternoon. When you're retired, there isn't much to do but read romances."

"I'd love to hear what you think about it. Nothing beats personal feedback from a reader."

"Will do. Thank you, honey."

Samantha was so tired on their way home that she almost fell asleep in Chris's car. She had eaten too much of the cake.

Chris parked on her driveway and tapped her on the shoulder.

"Hey sleepyhead, should I carry you to the bed like a sleeping princess?"

"It wouldn't hurt."

To Samantha's surprise, he took her in his strong arms and carried her to the door.

"The keys?" he asked.

"They're in my purse. Let me stand."

She fished for the keys and opened the door. Chris picked her up again. She placed her hands on his neck. He carried her over the doorstep as if they were a newlywed couple.

Winston welcomed them with a happy bark and followed them to the bedroom. Chris laid her down at the bed and took off her shoes. She felt drowsiness and yawned.

"Sweet dreams, Samantha." Chris gave her a light kiss in the lips and both cheeks.

"Good night, Chris."

She closed her eyes. She still saw his kind bearded face until sleep finally claimed her.

Chapter 10

Victoria checked her phone and saw it was five. She had to talk with Chris, had to explain to him that he would never find anyone better than her. Chris was hers, and Victoria always got what she wanted. The stupid old bitch wouldn't take him from her.

She left her home and went to the forest. If it was five on Saturday, Chris had to be taking a walk with Elsa. Victoria would have a chance to talk with him in private.

She followed the main trail and took a smaller trail leading to the bench. Three years ago, they kissed there for the first time. She would remember this warm July evening forever. It was the day she realized she had met the man of her dreams.

"Hey, Chris. I knew I would find you here."

Chris sat on the bench and petted Elsa. He was as handsome as always, well-dressed even on a walk with his dog. She approached the bench. Elsa ignored her.

"What do you want?"

"Why are you so nervous, sweetheart?"

"Stop calling me sweetheart. What did you think at the café?"

"Let bygones be bygones. I wanted to see you. I miss you."

"See me for what? Do I have to explain it to you once again we're no longer a couple?"

He was angry. But he would come around. He would see her for who she had always been. She only had to be patient.

"Stop following me. And leave Samantha alone."

Victoria clenched her fists and pursed her lips.

"So she did tell you that I paid her a little visit. What a weasel."

"Stop calling her that. You know nothing about her. What do you want from me?"

"Me? Nothing. I just want you to accept my love."

"Accept your love? Do you even hear what you're saying?"

"Chris, there was something between us."

"It was. No longer is."

"Yet you're still single, three years later. I know you want me. I can see it in your eyes," she said, tracing his forearm with her fingers.

"Stop it." He pushed her hand away. Elsa gave him her paw, as if she was trying to calm him down.

"Don't you remember how we kissed here for the first time? How madly in love we were? Why can't we start all over?"

"I don't love you, Victoria. I don't want to start all over. I'm done with you."

Victoria heard heavy footsteps coming from behind her. The stupid wolf dog ran toward them with his tongue hanging out the side of his mouth. In the distance between the trees, she saw the stupid old bitch. She was close enough to see them together.

Victoria pushed Chris to the tree with all her might. She covered the shocked look on his face with her long blonde hair and kissed him. He managed to push her away in seconds, but it was enough. Samantha was already running away, tears probably already flowing down her stupid old face.

"I will always wait for you, Chris."

Chapter 11

When Samantha saw Victoria kissing with Chris, she couldn't believe her eyes. Yet it happened, and it wasn't just a friendly kiss. She didn't even have it in her to call Winston back. She just left, hoping that he would notice she was gone and follow her.

That's what she got for thinking a younger guy would really choose her over a young busty blonde. He was just like Robert. Tears streamed down her face as she walked into her house and collapsed on the sofa.

The doorbell rang.

"Samantha, open the door, please. We need to talk," Chris said. He had to run after her. What for, she didn't understand.

"Leave me alone."

"Samantha, it was Victoria who kissed me."

"Stop lying and go away. You sound like my ex-husband."

"Samantha, please."

"Go, or I'll call the police."

"Samantha…"

"You heard me."

She heard him turn around and descend the porch steps. Samantha plodded to her writing room. Writing had always helped her escape the world. Perhaps it had been a misunderstanding, after all, but she wasn't ready to talk just yet.

Her phone rang a few hours later in the evening.

"Stop calling me. I don't want to talk with you," she yelled to the phone.

"Samantha?"

"I'm sorry Sarah, I… I didn't check who was calling."

"Samantha, what is going on?"

"It's nothing."

"Nothing? Don't lie to your sister."

"I saw Chris kissing Victoria."

"You saw what? When?"

"Today, a few hours ago. I was on a walk with Winston. And I saw them kissing in the forest."

"Are you sure it was him?"

"It was him. Elsa, his dog, was with him."

"Why would he do that? You said you had such a nice dinner a few days ago."

"I don't know. I guess he realized a forty-something woman is no match for a twenty-something girl."

"I… I don't know what to say."

Samantha had rarely heard confusion in Sarah's voice.

"Maybe you should talk with him? It could have been a misunderstanding," Sarah said.

"I need some time to think about it."

"Why don't you come to L.A. for a couple days? We'll go shopping, go to a nice restaurant, have some fun. Then you will think of what to do."

"What about Winston?"

"What about him? Take him with you. That's not a problem."

"Sarah, he's almost as tall as your daughter."

"It's okay. We'll find a place for him."

"Adam will be pissed off."

"He won't. He's on a business trip. Back next Tuesday."

"Sarah, I don't know. I… Let me think about it, okay? I'll call you back tomorrow."

"Okay. Samantha, do you want to talk about Chris?"

"Not now. I need to be alone. Thank you for calling."

***

The next day, Samantha worked like a horse, trying to focus on the work instead of thinking about Chris. When she couldn't concentrate on her work any longer, she closed her laptop, took a shower and went to bed. Even though she worked the entire day, she found herself unable to fall sleep.

Samantha hadn't had a sleepless night since Robert told her he wanted a divorce. This time, she at least had Winston to keep her company. He lay beside her in the bed as if he were just a puppy, not a dog who took up more than half of the bed.

"What do I do, Winston?" she asked him. Winston stared at her, a sad look in his eyes.

Samantha finally fell asleep around seven in the morning, right after a brief walk with Winston. It wasn't until noon when she woke up and noticed something lying on her front porch. She picked up a small manila envelope with her name on it.

Samantha sat at her couch in the living room and opened the envelope to see a handwritten letter from Chris.

Samantha,

I'm sorry I can't tell you this in person.

I'm sad that it had to end this way. I thought my love for Victoria was gone. I really did. But when I met with her to tell her to stay away from you, it all came back.

Four years ago, I kissed her for the first time on this bench. Three years ago, we broke up. I haven't really had a woman in my life since Victoria. Two days ago, when I saw her in the forest when you saw us, I realized she was the only one.

I hope we can still be friends.

Chris

Samantha sat on the couch. What a jerk. She had always thought it was impossible to top off Robert's arrogance. Chris had set a new record. And to think she wanted to give him a chance to explain himself.

Tears welled in her eyes. She picked up the phone.

"Sarah, can I come? I need to get away."

Chapter 12

Winston enjoyed exploring Sarah's house and playing with her daughter. The trip did little good for Samantha, though.

She spent a lot of time with her sister. They went to the park, they went shopping, they had a great dinner at Samantha's favorite place and watched her favorite movies at night. Sarah meant well, but Samantha knew nothing could help when you were betrayed by yet another man. Betrayed in almost the same manner, at that.

When she returned to Maple Hills, she realized she could no longer live there.

If Winston had any health problems, she would have to go to Chris or drive thirty miles to the nearest town with a veterinary clinic. If she went to the forest, there was a chance she would meet him there. If she wanted to go to the store, she might meet him or his aunt there.

If you build a relationship in a small town and it goes south, you can't avoid each other as you could do back in L.A.

She opened her laptop and started looking for a new place to live. She checked small towns away from everything and made a list of seven potential places where she could move. She even considered moving to Canada. She had enough savings to buy a farmhouse and live with Winston with no other people in sight. Just like an old woman, but what the hell. She wasn't going to be disappointed again.

Winston interrupted her research by putting his paw on her lap. He looked at her with a begging gaze.

"I'm so sorry buddy. I completely forgot about your walk. Let's go."

Samantha took a different route in the forest, hoping that she wouldn't cross paths with Chris. It was five, the time when his clinic was open, but she figured it was better to be safe than sorry.

Samantha let Winston loose. The dog ran away after a squirrel. She put hands into her pockets, lowered her head and returned her thoughts to her plan to leave town. If she was quick about it, she could find a new place and pack all her things in less than a week. Less than a week of avoiding Chris and his aunt. It was doable. She didn't have any other option, anyway.

She heard barking of two dogs and stopped dead in her tracks. Winston came back with a beagle running around his legs. The small dog looked ridiculous standing beside her giant Irish Wolfhound. A second later, Chris's aunt Florence emerged from a tree-covered trail at Samantha's right.

"Samantha, honey, what a coincidence."

"Hello, Florence. I… I must get going." Samantha turned around and began to stride off.

"Sweetheart, I think we need to talk."

Samantha turned on her heels and gazed at Florence.

"Talk about what?"

"About you and Chris. He's been so sad recently. Something has happened between the two of you."

"Why don't you ask him?"

"He doesn't want to talk with me about it."

"It's not my problem."

"Honey, he's been talking about you ever since he met you. He hasn't talked about anyone like this for ages."

"It seems he got bored."

Florence raised an eyebrow.

"What do you mean?"

"I saw him with Victoria. They were kissing."

"Victoria? That impolite girl? No, I don't believe that."

"I saw Elsa with him. Besides, he wrote me a letter."

"A letter?"

"He left me a letter on my porch on Monday morning. He said he's back with Victoria."

"Monday morning? At what hour?"

"What does it matter?"

"Honey, please answer my question."

"I took a walk with Winston at seven in the morning. So later than that. Somewhere between seven and noon, I'd say."

"I have no idea what is going on, but Chris did not leave this letter."

"What are you talking about?"

"We left town together at six in the morning on Monday. He went to an annual veterinary convention while I was shopping in the city."

"He could have written it before and gave it to someone else to deliver it."

"Sweetheart, could you show me this letter? I know his handwriting."

"I… Well, okay."

***

"It wasn't written by Chris. It was written by a woman, most likely." Florence gave the letter back to Samantha.

"And how do you know that?"

"Honey, I was a high school teacher for forty years. I can tell your future by your handwriting."

"Do you want to say that someone else wrote this letter and delivered it here? Why would she do that?"

"To make you hate him?"

"Who would do that?"

"Victoria?"

"I... I don't know. Could she really be so... so cold?"

"You better talk with Chris. It's time for me to go, anyway. Oh, and thank you for the book. I really liked it."

Florence left Samantha's house with her beagle trotting right beside her leg. Winston didn't even bother to get up and say goodbye to his dog friend. He appeared preoccupied with Samantha.

"What do I do now, Winston?" The dog just stared at her with a thoughtful look on his face, as if he was considering his options.

Chapter 13

The next day, when Samantha sat down to write a new chapter of her new novel, she realized she didn't have her favorite green tea. Fortunately, it was already three in the afternoon, so she wouldn't run into Chris at the store. She kept avoiding him, unsure if she should trust him again. She had been betrayed by a man once, and she didn't want it to happen again.

When she got back home thirty minutes later, Winston was gone.

This time she didn't waste her time and went directly into the forest. An hour later and with a sore throat after shouting for Winston a gazillion times, she realized the dog wasn't in the forest or she would have already found him.

She went back home to grab her car keys. If the dog wasn't in the forest, he had to be at Chris's place. Just what she needed.

When she parked at Chris's driveway, the dog was nowhere in sight. She rang the doorbell. Nobody answered, not even Elsa with her barking. Samantha took out her cell phone to call Chris. The battery was dead.

She hopped back into her car and drove to the clinic. When she pulled into the parking lot, she was surprised to see a "closed" sign on the door. It was five, so it should have been opened for another hour or two.

Samantha drove to the animal shelter to ask James and Melinda. If there was anybody in the town who knew everything about lost dogs, it was James and Melinda.

"Chris is looking for you. Winston is with him," James said.

Samantha rushed back to her car and headed home.

When she parked on her driveway, she saw Elsa and Winston playing in the backyard. She felt an immediate relief, until she noticed Chris sitting in her garden chair. When Chris saw Samantha leave her car, he rose up from the chair and walked to her car.

"Hi Samantha."

"Where were you? I looked for you… I mean for Winston, for hours." She pointed at the dog who was so busy playing with Elsa he didn't even bother to say hello to her.

"Imagine this… A patient leaves my office. And who do I see sitting right beside the door? My dear Winston… with Elsa."

Samantha told Chris where she had been looking for Winston.

"I brought Winston here, but he didn't want to stay. So I took him and Elsa to the forest to look for you. Then I went to the shelter. And then I just got back here and sat down in the chair hoping you'd be back soon."

"Thank you, Chris." She wanted him to hug her, but at the same time she was afraid to open her heart yet again.

"Don't we have something to talk about? I read the letter."

"You did what?"

"I left out one part from my story… When I saw Winston at my clinic, he had a manila envelope in his mouth."

"Victoria's letter?"

"Do you believe me now? Victoria faked the letter. She faked the kiss, too. Everything to keep me away from you."

"Chris, I'm not ready for another disappointment."

"I won't disappoint you."

"My ex-husband had been known to say the same things. And then he left me."

"I have never met a woman like you in my entire life."

She stared at him, unsure what to say. Risk yet another disappointment or trust that this time it would be different?

"Samantha, I'll do everything to regain your trust."

His pleading eyes melted her heart. There was something in his eyes that made her realize he fought for her. She was important to him.

"Please kiss me," she whispered.

He grabbed her by the forearm and pulled her to him. His lips met hers and they kissed with wild passion, as if they haven't seen each other for years.

"I missed you so much," Samantha said.

"I missed you, too." His gentle hand brushed her hair.

"I read your book," he whispered to her ear.

She pulled away from the hug to look into his eyes.

"You did? And what do you think about it?"

"I loved it, but I think the last scene needs a bit reworking. You know, the one in the bedroom. I can show you how to fix it."

Samantha looked at his thoughtful face and burst out laughing.

"What? You could really use some help rewriting this scene," he said, pulling her by the hand into her home.

Chapter 14

When Chris entered Black Bean Café, several people sent him a wink. Victoria had been spreading rumors, there was no other explanation. He ignored their gazes and walked over to the counter.

“Hi, Larry. Is Victoria around?”

“Nope. She’s no longer working here.” There was a hint of amusement in his voice.

“What happened?”

“Your aunt hasn’t told you?”

“No. What happened?”

“Yesterday she came here and yelled at Victoria in front of the entire café. Said something about faking a letter and destroying your love life. If you only saw Victoria’s reddened face,” he chuckled. “She ran away. Her notice was on the front door in the morning.”

Chris left the café, got into his car and drove to Victoria’s home.

He rang the doorbell. Victoria opened the door. Her face was tired, as if she had a sleepless night. Chris noticed moving boxes standing in the hallway.

“We should talk,” he said.

Victoria nodded and let him in. They walked to the living room with a lone sofa and armchair standing in the middle of the room. Victoria sat at the sofa. Chris chose the armchair.

“I’m so sorry, Chris. I made a mistake.”

Chris looked at her with astonishment. Did she really just apologize? Out of all the things he would expect from Victoria it was the last thing on the list.

“You’ve probably already heard what happened yesterday in the café.”

"I have."

"Well, there's not much to add. Your aunt was right. I only thought about myself, not about you."

Chris sat in silence and weighed his words. Had his Aunt really accomplished something he couldn't accomplish for the last three years?

"I was a bitch to you and made myself the laughingstock of the town. Chris, can you forgive me?"

Chris gazed deep into her eyes. She really felt guilty.

"I... I forgive you."

She exhaled a long breath. Her face muscles relaxed.

"Friends?" She extended her hand.

"Friends."

They shook hands. Chris rose up and walked down the hallway to the front door. Victoria followed him. He opened the door and turned around.

"I wish you the best, Chris. I hope you'll be happy with Samantha."

"Good luck, Vic."

***

Samantha hung up the phone.

"This will be the last one. Everything scheduled for tomorrow," she said.

"Thank God. I don't mind the puppies, but seven was definitely a little too much," Chris said.

They were sitting in Samantha's living room. A litter of seven gray puppies with white and brown spots lay down in a makeshift bed Chris made from a plastic crate and old blankets. Proud parents, Winston and Elsa, guarded the puppies day and night.

"Now that we took care of the puppies, there's one more thing we need to talk about," she said.

"What's up, honey?"

"Elsa has been practically living with me for the last two months."

"I will take her home tomorrow."

"No, that's not what I meant. I was thinking that maybe… maybe you should move in."

Chris looked at her with wide eyes.

"My home and backyard are bigger than yours and our dogs are an item. It would make things easier," she continued. Doubt crept into her mind. Did she want too much commitment from him?

"Samantha, there's nothing in the world that would make me happier than waking up beside you every single day."

If Samantha had any doubts about his feelings, they were all gone the instant he gave her a passionate kiss and pulled her in a tight embrace.

Every Dog Has Its Day

Chapter 1

"I've been walking the woods for hours. No trace of Lucky," Laura said to her friend Samantha over the phone. She couldn't keep her voice from shaking.

"Laura, calm down. We'll find him. Have you checked the shelter?"

"I did. They'll let me know if they see him."

"Send me over a couple photos of Lucky. I'll make some posters. We'll hang them tomorrow first thing in the morning."

"Samantha, what about Winston? Could he find Lucky by smell?"

"I'll ask Chris. I think it's worth a shot. We can do that tomorrow, too. It's getting too dark to search for Lucky right now."

"Thank you, Samantha. I'll walk around the town once again before it gets completely dark."

Laura reached for a leather jacket hanging on a wooden coat hook near the door and found herself putting on a yellow slicker by mistake.

Hour by hour, she had been growing more and more desperate because of Lucky's disappearance. She would walk around the town again. She would find him. She had to. Everything would be all right soon.

Laura took off the slicker and put on the jacket. She closed the door with a thump.

She wandered the streets of the town shouting her dog's name every few seconds. To hell with people looking at her like a crazy person. She had to find Lucky.

Laura circled the entire town, walking the streets adjacent to the woods and the streets right in the center. Nobody had seen Lucky.

One hour later, she decided it was time to head home. The dog couldn't be in town. He had to be in the woods, but it was too dark to go there right now. She walked back to her home, hoping that Lucky would be waiting for her on the front porch.

He wasn't.

Laura opened the door and went to the kitchen. She took a chair standing by the kitchen table and brought it to the window overlooking the street in front of her home. She would wait for Lucky. He would be back soon. He had to. Your best friend couldn't just disappear like that.

Chapter 2

Richard left his home too late for his usual jog in the forest. It was getting dark, and he was still at least fifteen minutes from the edge of the woods. He could still make out the trail, but with each minute it was getting less and less visible. He felt as if the forest was taking the trail from under his feet, trying to swallow him into the darkness.

He felt the temptation to run faster, but he knew that would be dangerous. He wouldn't see roots, holes and any other obstacles on his way. The last thing he wanted was to twist his ankle in the middle of the woods when it was getting dark.

Richard turned left to the main trail leading to the town when he heard whining coming from the woods at the right. He stopped in his tracks and strained his ears. The sound came from inside the forest.

He walked toward the source of the noise, careful not to make too much sound. It could be a dog, or it could be a boar or something worse. He saw a large dark shape on the ground between the pines with something white on its front. It wasn't a boar. It was a dog.

He approached the shape. A large black dog with a white chest and rust colored markings on its face and legs lay on the forest floor. The dog had cuts on its front and back left paw as if it had been attacked by a wild animal. A small trail of blood led to the place where the dog lay.

"Who did this to you?" Richard asked. The dog raised its head and whined.

Richard squatted to inspect the wounds. It was too dark to tell how badly the dog was wounded, but he was sure the dog would never reach the town in this condition.

He placed his hands under the dog's massive belly and took him in his muscular arms. It had to weigh at least one hundred pounds. Richard was glad he had been working hard at the gym.

The dog looked at him with a begging gaze and whined. Taking small and careful steps, almost as if he was holding a tray full of food, Richard carried the dog to the main trail that was almost invisible in the darkness around them.

One hour later, he carried the dog into his bedroom. He took an old red plaid wool blanket from the drawer and laid the dog on it.

In full light, he could see the animal had been bitten in a few places, but it was its paws that were wounded the most. Richard noticed it was already past ten, long after the clinic's opening hours. He had to clean the wounds by himself.

He went to the bathroom and took out a small bucket. While the water was filling the bucket, he opened the drawer and grabbed the first aid kit. He took the supplies back to the bedroom. The dog raised its head and whined, as if begging for help.

Richard sat down near the dog and cleaned its wounds with cotton pads dipped in lukewarm water mixed with soap. Fortunately, the wounds weren't as dirty as he was worried they would be. Based on his limited medical experience, they shouldn't fester. The dog was lucky; there was no doubt about it.

When he was done cleaning the wounds, he bandaged the ones on the dog's paws and gauzed the wounds on its side and back. Then he brought a bowl of water. The dog guzzled the water as if it hasn't drunk anything for the entire day.

Richard looked at the animal and realized he hadn't checked if the dog had a tag. He removed its collar and examined the clean brown leather. No tag, nothing else to help him find the owner.

Richard put the collar away. The dog observed him with its head lying on the blanket and its eyes looking up. He patted the dog on its head. It was soft and smooth. He was surprised to see that despite its condition, the dog wagged its tail.

"It's okay buddy, you should rest."

The dog gazed at him for the last time and closed its eyes. It was snoring in seconds. Richard looked at the bowl and realized how thirsty he was. He went to the kitchen and grabbed a cold bottle of water. It was just what he needed after a long run and carrying a one hundred pound dog for over two miles.

Tomorrow, he would have to find the owner. He was glad that he had an afternoon shift at the gym. It would give him plenty of time to ask around and return the dog to its owner.

He went back to his bedroom to check on the dog. It was still in a deep sleep, its snoring penetrating the quiet room. Richard walked to the bathroom and took a shower. When he was clean and dressed in his pajamas, he returned to his bedroom. He lay on the edge of the bed, right above the snoring animal.

Richard extended his arm and stroked the dog. It moved from lying on its stomach to lying on its side. Richard moved his hand across the dog's side, careful to avoid touching its gauzed wounds. He realized it was his first night in two years that he wouldn't spent alone. The dog's presence was comforting, even if it meant he would have to get up early the next day to find the owner.

Richard fell asleep on his stomach, with his left hand on the dog's side.

Chapter 3

"Laura, I have good news for you."

"Oh my God, Melinda, please tell me it's Lucky!" Laura shouted to the phone.

"Yes, it's Lucky. Mr. Richard Tanner found him."

"Where's Lucky?"

"He's at Richard's place. Please come to the shelter. He'll take you to his home."

"I'll be there right away."

Laura put on her sports shoes and ran to the kitchen to grab the car keys. She dashed outside and jumped in her car. Laura sped through the empty streets hoping Tom wouldn't be patrolling them so early in the morning. She glanced at the dashboard clock. It was six thirty.

Five minutes later, she pulled her car to a stop in a small dirt parking lot in front of the shelter's office. Melinda and a muscular brunet stood in front of the building talking with each other.

She hopped out her car and strode to the pair.

"Hi, Laura. Meet Mr. Richard Tanner." Melinda pointed to a thirty-something brawny brunet with black stubble on his face and deep brown eyes.

"Laura Rogers. Nice to meet you, Mr. Tanner."

"Nice to meet you, too. And please call me Richard."

"Richard, could you take me to Lucky?"

"Of course, please follow my car," he said. "See you Melinda, and thanks for your help."

Richard got into his gray Toyota Camry and pulled out of the parking lot and onto the street. Laura tailgated him, her gaze concentrated on sticking to his car as close as possible.

A few minutes later, they pulled into Richard's driveway in front of a white wooden house with an olive green roof. Richard got out of his car and motioned Laura to follow him. He opened the door and led her through a hallway to a well-lit spacious bedroom. Lucky lay on the blanket near the bed. When she entered the room, Lucky tried standing on its bandaged paws. Laura dashed to the dog to keep him from falling.

"Lucky! Oh my God, what happened to you?" She squatted and embraced Lucky in her arms. The dog wagged its tail in wide circles and licked her face.

"I was running in the forest yesterday and heard whining coming from the woods. That's where I found him. It seems he was attacked by something. I cleaned his wounds, but I think you should take him to a vet."

"I'll take him to Chris. How did you get him here? He can't even stand on his legs."

"I carried him."

"You carried him? He weighs one hundred and twenty pounds."

He shrugged.

Laura caressed Lucky's head and looked into his eyes. The joy she saw in his chestnut brown eyes filled her with exhilaration. Lucky was all right. Everything would be back to normal now that he was back with her.

"I don't know how to thank you, Richard. If it wasn't for you, he might be… I don't even want to think about it." She shuddered.

"He was lucky I left home later than usual. The name indeed fits him."

"It's the luckiest dog on Earth. Right, Lucky?" Laura said, embracing the dog once again.

"I think we should take him to a vet."

"We? Richard, I don't want to take advantage of your kindness."

"How are you going to carry him to the car and then back home? He can barely walk."

"I... You have a point."

"My shift starts at noon. Let me call Chris."

While Richard called Chris, Laura inspected Lucky's wounds. His front and back left paws were bandaged. He had a large gauze on his side, a small gauze on his stomach, and another one on his neck. She sobbed. If she kept him on a leash, he wouldn't have ran away and everything would be okay.

"We have an appointment at the clinic in thirty minutes."

"I can't thank you enough, Richard."

"It's okay, Laura. I'm glad I can help."

She gazed at his face. His dark brown eyes, high cheekbones and light stubble complemented his olive complexion. She found a strange sense of comfort in looking at him.

She turned her attention back to Lucky, who had been licking his empty bowl.

"Let me refill it. He's already drunk everything I gave him an hour ago," Richard said.

Laura handed him the bowl. While Richard was gone, she looked around the bedroom. A king-size bed with beige bedding dominated the green-painted room. There was only one pillow on the bed.

On a nightstand near the bed, she saw a framed picture of an attractive thirty-something blonde woman with a pearly white smile. She was standing in front of a yacht, probably somewhere in Florida. She reminded Laura of herself. She had the same oval-shaped face and the same light blond color of hair. Even her eyes had a similar shade of blue.

Richard returned and sat criss-crossed beside her. He placed the bowl under Lucky's nose. Richard's wide arms bulged under his simple fitted black t-shirt. He smelled of soap. Its scent reminded Laura of something familiar she couldn't remember.

Richard stroked Lucky's head with sensitivity she didn't expect from such a masculine man.

"Good boy," he said. Lucky licked his hand.

Laura smiled. Richard had a way with dogs.

"Have you ever had a dog?" she asked.

"I had a German shepherd. He died three years ago."

"I'm sorry."

"I'm glad I could spend some time with Lucky. I guess I miss having a dog."

"Why don't you get one?"

"When my first dog died, I said to myself I would never have another dog. It was too painful to see him go. I'm not sure I'm ready for another dog."

"You have a way with dogs. I can see it in Lucky how he's looking at you."

"He's a fine dog. I've always loved large dogs. By the way, what breed is Lucky?"

"Bernese Mountain Dog."

"Interesting. I have never heard of it."

"It was originally kept as a farm dog. It's an outdoor dog, not well suited for city living. Fortunately we live pretty close to the woods. That's where I lost him." Her voice broke.

"It's okay, Laura, he's back with you."

"I'm so sorry to see him this way. I always let him loose. I don't know why he ran away yesterday."

"Something must have caught his attention. Anyway, he's okay now."

"What if he caught rabies?"

"He couldn't. An annual rabies vaccine is required by law so he had to get it."

"What about other illnesses?"

"Laura, don't think about it now. We'll go to Chris in a second. He'll check him and everything will be all right."

"I'm sorry, Richard. I… Lucky is my best friend. I don't know what I would do without him." She broke down and sobbed.

"It's okay, Laura, no need to apologize for anything."

He hugged her. She cried in his arms.

"I should have known better than let him loose so deep in the woods."

"Shhh…"

They sat at the floor near Lucky. Richard hugged her and gently stroked her back in a comforting manner.

"I think we should get going. We have the appointment in twenty minutes," he said.

Laura broke the hug. What was she thinking hugging a stranger like that? She hadn't been thinking straight.

Laura stood up and went to the bathroom to wash her face. Her blue eyes were reddened and her blond hair was disheveled. She licked her lips and tasted salt. Laura washed her face as best as she could and returned to the room.

Lucky lay on an unfolded blanket, ready to carry him out of the room. Richard sat beside Lucky and stroked his head.

"I'm ready," she said.

Richard patted the dog for the last time and stood up.

"Let's carry him on the blanket. Grab this end and I'll grab the other one." He walked behind Lucky to grab the end close to the dog's tail.

They carried Lucky to Laura's red Nissan Pathfinder and laid him on his side on the back seat. The dog was so huge that he took more than half of the space in the back.

"I'll follow you," Richard said and went to his car.

Laura backed the car out of his driveway and drove through Richard's neighborhood toward the main street leading to the clinic.

***

"The good news is that Richard did a great job cleaning the wounds," said Chris Green, the only veterinarian in the town. He smiled at Richard standing in the back of the room.

Laura hadn't seen Chris for a few weeks, even though he had been living with her close friend Samantha. His short brown hair and beard were disheveled. Richard had to wake him up when he called him to check up on Lucky.

"And the bad news?" she asked.

"The bad news is that he'll have to take it easy for the next two weeks or so. Ideally, he shouldn't walk at all for the next few days."

"Is there any risk of an illness or infection?"

"He was bit in numerous places, but like I said, Richard did a great job cleaning the wounds. Infection is not likely. I stitched the larger wounds."

"When would you like to check on him again?"

"Please come again on Thursday. And if there's anything that worries you, don't hesitate to call me – even late at night or early in the morning."

"Thank you, Chris. I appreciate your help. Could you please tell Samantha Lucky was found? I completely forgot to let her know."

"I've already told her when Richard called me."

"Thank you. I'm sorry I didn't let her know earlier."

"It's okay, you were rattled."

Laura paid the bill and took the medications Chris gave her for Lucky. Richard carried the dog from the examination table to the blanket on the floor. He and Laura grabbed the ends of the blanket and left the office. They put Lucky on the back seat of Laura's car.

"Thank you again, Richard. I don't know what I would do without you."

"You want to carry Lucky by yourself from your car to your home? Let me help you."

"Richard, you really don't have to."

"But I would like to help. Please, let me help you. He shouldn't walk and you won't carry him by yourself like that."

"I guess you have a point. Okay."

Ten minutes later, they pulled into her driveway. She parked her car close to the front door. Her arms were sore from carrying Lucky. She had no idea how Richard had managed to carry Lucky by himself for at least a mile, if not more.

He got out of his car and opened the door on the driver's side of her car. If he wasn't dressed in a simple t-shirt, he would look like a gentleman helping his lady out of the car before a ball.

"Thank you," she said.

Laura opened the door to her house while Richard entered her car to accompany Lucky. She heard him talking to Lucky and smiled at the sight of a huge muscular man talking to a dog.

She got into the car to grab the ends of the blanket under Lucky's tail. Richard grabbed the ends closer to the door. They carried the dog to her house and into her bedroom.

"Let's lay him over there in his bed." Laura pointed to a brown and beige bed in the corner of the room. It was Lucky's favorite place, and her office as well. She would have an eye on him at all times.

She went to the kitchen and brought his bowl of water and a bowl of food. She was surprised when Lucky raised his head and started eating. Just a minute ago he looked ready to sleep.

"It's a positive sign, isn't it?" she asked.

"For sure it is. Animals don't eat when they're ill. I guess he's feeling better."

"Thank God."

"Laura, I must get going."

"Thank you, Richard. And sorry for what happened at your home."

"It's okay, Laura, you really don't have to apologize. I'm glad I could help. Oh, and by the way, please call me on Thursday. I will help you carry Lucky."

"Richard, it's really not necessary. I can manage."

"Let me help. I'd love to see how he feels two days from now."

"What about your wife? Won't she be mad you're helping a random woman with her dog?"

"She… Olivia passed away two years ago."

"I… I'm sorry. I saw the picture in your bedroom."

"I still haven't managed to find a different place for it."

They stared at each other in awkward silence.

"Well, like I said, I'll be glad to help you. Please call me on Thursday."

They exchanged phone numbers. Richard squatted near Lucky who had just finished eating his food.

"I'm glad you're okay, buddy," Richard said and patted him on the head.

The dog wagged its tail and tried licking Richard's face.

"Yuck. You just ate, man."

Laura laughed at Richard's disgusted face and Lucky's efforts to lick him.

"Maybe next time when you brush your teeth, brother," he said and stood up.

Laura accompanied Richard to the door.

"Thank you again, Richard. When can I call you on Thursday?"

"I have a morning shift. I'll be back home at one o'clock, so we can go to the clinic at two."

"Sounds great. See you."

"Bye."

Richard descended the steps of the porch and got inside his car. He backed the car out of her driveway and waved at her. She waved back and went inside to check on Lucky. The light scent of Richard's soap lingered in the air. She liked it.

Chapter 4

"Would you like tea or coffee?" Laura said.

"Green tea would be fine. Thanks," Samantha said.

Laura turned the kettle on. She took two tea mugs from the drawer and put them on the countertop. She placed tea bags into the mugs and waited for the kettle to finish boiling.

"So, what exactly happened to Lucky? How was he found?"

"Richard Tanner was running in the forest in the evening. He heard Lucky's whining and carried him to his house."

"*Carried* him?"

"I know. Lucky weighs about one hundred and twenty pounds."

"Ah, I forgot! Chris told me about him once. He's a personal trainer at the gym."

"A fitness coach, huh? He certainly looked like one."

"If I remember right, Chris told me he's been working as a coach for at least five years. They know each other from the gym. Anyway, what happened later?"

"He cleaned Lucky's wounds. Chris said he did a great job."

"That's what Chris told me, too. He said that if it wasn't for Richard, Lucky might not have been so lucky."

"Oh God."

"Don't think about it, Laura. Lucky's back and he'll be right as rain soon."

The kettle whistled and Laura poured the water into the mugs. She put a tea thermometer into one of the mugs.

"75 degrees Celsius, as always," Samantha said.

"Right on."

Laura put the cooling mugs on the wooden kitchen table and sat at the chair.

"So, what do you think about Richard?" Samantha asked.

"He's kind and has a way with dogs."

"And?"

"And what?"

"Laura, I know you enough to tell when there's *something* on your mind."

"*Something?*"

"He helped you with Lucky and all, but I think there's something more about this story. Am I right?"

"Samantha, life isn't a romance."

"Laura, out of all the people, you don't have to remind *me* of it. I still know you haven't told me something."

"Okay, okay, I give up. I think he's handsome. There, satisfied?"

"And what are you going to do about it?"

"Nothing."

"Chris told me he wants to check Lucky in two days. Will Richard help you carry Lucky there?"

"He will."

"Oh, look at you. Isn't it convenient?"

"Samantha, please."

Laura removed the thermometer and put tea bags in the mugs.

"Three minutes," Samantha said.

"As usual." Laura set a white egg timer to three minutes.

"Back to the topic. What about Richard?"

"Samantha, he's widowed. I saw the photo of his deceased wife on his nightstand. He wasn't happy to talk about it."

"That's understandable. But still, he doesn't have to help you. You could have asked Chris to check on Lucky here."

"I… I didn't want to bother him."

"Or maybe you wanted a reason to meet with Richard again?"

"Samantha, please."

"Yet, there's something more to the story, isn't it?"

"I liked how he touched Lucky. How sensitive he was and how kind he was toward me. I… I broke down in tears when I saw Lucky. Richard hugged me. He had such a comforting touch."

Samantha nodded. "What happened later?"

"Nothing. We had to get up and go to the clinic."

"Still, something happened between you."

"Samantha, it was just a comforting hug."

"Perhaps it was, but it doesn't explain that he wants to help you when you no longer need his help."

"He's just kind. I think he likes Lucky, and Lucky likes him."

"And he likes Laura. And Laura likes him."

"Samantha, stop it. I've been single for too many years. I have no intention of changing it."

"It's never too late to shake things up, Laura. Never too late."

Chapter 5

"Let me help you," Richard said. They helped Lucky get up and lie on the blanket they put near the bed to carry him to the car.

"Let's go, buddy," Laura said.

They carried Lucky to Laura's car and put him in the back. Richard started walking to his car when Laura stopped him.

"Richard, wouldn't it be more economical to take just one car? You can drive with me."

"Sure," he said. He got inside the car with her.

They drove to the clinic in silence, both of them unsure of what to say to each other. Ten minutes later, Laura pulled over in the parking lot of the clinic. Richard got outside first and circled the car to open the door on her side. . She liked his antiquated manners.

"Let's go see the doctor, brother," Richard said to Lucky.

Yet again, they carried Lucky together to the clinic. Laura swore that if she had to do it a few times more, she would have larger biceps than Richard.

Chris opened the door to the clinic for them and motioned them to get inside the office. They laid Lucky on the examination table. This time, he wasn't as calm as before and wanted to get up and leave the room.

"Not so quick, Lucky. We need to check on you," Chris said.

For the next five minutes, Chris examined Lucky. He measured his temperature, pulse and respiration rate. He inspected Lucky head-to-toe, checking his eyes, ears, mouth, belly, legs, feet and joints. He also checked on his wounds.

"The wounds are healing well. I don't have any concerns about his health."

"Thank God." Laura breathed a sigh of relief.

"I think tomorrow you can let him walk a little. Just a little. A walk around the backyard will be fine."

"Of course."

"And please come with him again in five days. Tuesday or Wednesday will be fine. I need to remove his stitches."

"Tuesday works fine for me, unless it's better to wait for one more day."

"No, Tuesday is great."

"Perfect. See you on Tuesday then, Chris."

"Sure. And remember, if you notice anything worrying, give me a call."

"Thank you. I appreciate it."

They carried Lucky back to the car. Chris opened the door on the driver's side and motioned her to get in. She smiled at him.

They drove back to her home and carried Lucky to the bedroom.

"See you, buddy," Richard said and stroked Lucky's head. He stood up and turned around to leave.

"Richard, would you like to have some coffee or tea with me?"

"I… I would love to. And tea would be fine."

"Lucky, you stay here and get some sleep," Laura said to Lucky. He raised his head as if nodding and put it back down.

Laura walked with Richard to the kitchen. He sat at the kitchen table while Laura poured water into the kettle.

"Black, green, white?"

"Green would be perfect."

She turned the kettle on and retrieved two mugs from the drawer. She opened another drawer and took two tea bags of green tea from the black and white metal tin.

"So, what do you do?" Richard asked.

"I'm a freelance writer. I write articles for websites and blogs."

"That's interesting. Any specialties?"

"Real estate and finance, mostly. Not that interesting, but it pays the bills."

"Good for you."

"What about you?" Laura asked.

"I'm a personal trainer at the Maple Hills Gym. The one around the car wash."

"Yeah, I know the place. I was there once and never came back. Long walks with Lucky serve me much better than the torture you offer there."

Richard laughed. His laugh had a deep penetrating note. It broke the tension between them she had felt since their silent drive to the clinic.

"To each his own, I guess. As long as my clients keep exercising, I don't care if they do it at home, in the woods or at the gym."

"That's a healthy approach. When I was there, a huge bald guy told me I needed to do squats three times per week if I wanted to shape my… my bum."

"That's probably Mark. He's big on squats. He could do them all day long."

The kettle boiled. Laura poured the water into the mugs and put a tea thermometer in one of the mugs.

"What's that?"

"It's a tea thermometer."

"Seriously? Why would you use it?"

"Green tea tastes best in seventy five degrees Celsius. Infuse it in boiling hot water and it will taste horribly."

"Horribly? That's how I always drink my green tea."

"Today you're going to drink it the right way. Prepare to be blown away."

"I can't wait."

"It will be ready in about five minutes. Tell me something more about you. Why a personal trainer?"

"I like helping people. That's really all there is to it. It's a very satisfying job."

"I see. Torturing people has its appeal."

He laughed. Laura felt comfortable around him. She liked people who could take a joke.

"What about you? Why freelance writing?"

"I like working at home and working at my own pace. It would kill me to wake up at seven and go to a nine to five job."

"I understand."

"And, besides, I enjoy independence. I can't take orders from other people."

"That explains why you hate the gym. You can't be the boss there."

"Exactly."

"Then it's good you never came back. Mark hates people who don't listen to his advice."

Laura checked the thermometer and removed it from the mug. She put tea bags in the mugs and set the kitchen egg timer to three minutes.

"What's that about?"

"For the perfect taste, you need to wait three minutes. No more, no less."

"Alright, boss. I better not argue with you."

Laura laughed. She liked Richard more and more. He could take a joke and be quite playful, too.

"I have never asked you… How long have you had Lucky?"

"It will be three years in August. Huh, time flies by so fast."

"It does."

They sat in silence for two minutes. Laura played with the egg timer, while Richard inspected the thermometer.

The alarm went off and Laura removed the tea bags from the mugs.

"You can drink it now."

"No other step? Like taking a sip, spilling the rest and infusing it again?"

"Not this time. We'll start with the basics," she said. The word "start" lingered in her mind as if she said something wrong.

Richard took a small sip.

"It's incredible," he said.

"Oh, stop joking. You can't tell the taste with just one sip. You'll tell me what you think when you finish the cup." She sent him a playful smile.

They sat in silence and sipped the tea. Light shone through the wide kitchen window and illuminated Richard's face. Laura glanced at his rough features and black stubble. He raised his gaze to her face and looked deep into her eyes. She felt a shiver jolting through her spine.

"I'll check on Lucky. I'll be back in a second," she said and left the kitchen.

She went to the bedroom. Lucky was sprawled on his bed. She squatted near him and stroked his back. She was glad to see him getting better. In no time, she would be able to return to their regular walks in the woods. Their lonely walks.

Her mind shifted to Richard. What was that in the kitchen? She wasn't sure why she had felt so queasy when he looked at her. He would be out of her life soon. Things would go back to normal. But she was no longer sure what had been normal. Their conversation in the kitchen felt somehow right to her, as if something had been taken from her many years ago and returned only now. And it sure felt normal.

Richard knocked on the doorframe and entered the room. "Is everything okay?"

"Yes. I just wanted to check on Lucky, make sure he's comfortable," she lied. "Let's go back to the kitchen."

They returned to the kitchen and sat at the table.

"I was thinking about what you told me two days ago."

"About what?"

"About me having a way with dogs. And that I should get a dog."

"And?"

"And I'm debating whether I should get one. The night spent with Lucky made me realize how empty my home is."

"That's what I felt the night Lucky was gone."

"I'm sorry. I could have asked Chris to come and help me find the owner."

"No, it's okay. I was just saying I know what you feel. So, what's your decision?"

"I'm not sure yet. I don't know if I'm ready to get involved in a new relationship."

Laura felt as if something pricked her heart. "R... Relationship?"

"I mean a relationship with a new dog. I'm sorry. It's stupid to think of dogs as of people."

"No, it's kind of sweet to put it this way. I know what you mean by it."

"Anyway, the jury is still out. I thought I would ask you what you think about it."

"I think you should take your time. Definitely don't go to the shelter before you make the final decision."

"I'm not sure if I would be able to give enough attention to a dog. When Olivia was still alive, we split the responsibilities. We had different schedules so we could take Julian on long walks every single day."

"What's your schedule now? How long are your shifts?"

"It depends. Usually six to eight hours."

"Your schedule isn't a problem, then. What's the real problem?"

"I... I'm sorry, I shouldn't have asked you."

"Richard, if there's anything you'd like to talk about, please tell me. It's the least I can do to thank you for saving Lucky's life."

"Have you ever loved someone with all your heart?"

"I... No. I've been single my entire life. Unless you count Lucky." Her attempt to clear the air with a joke didn't work. Richard sent her a solemn look.

"The last time I had a dog, Olivia was still alive. All my memories of Julian are somehow related to her. If I get a new dog, it would be like starting with a clean slate."

"Isn't it a good thing to ignore the past and start all over?"

"It's not that simple. At least not for me. You saw the picture on the nightstand."

"I'm sorry, Richard. I don't know what to say."

"It's okay. Anyway, that's why I'm not sure. I guess I'll take your advice and go slowly."

Laura sent him a feeble smile. She felt so much pain hiding between his words.

"By the way, the tea is indeed much better than when I use boiling hot water. From now on, I will use your recipe, boss," he said in a casual tone, as if they haven't exchanged a word about his deceased wife.

"I'm glad to hear that. Another barbarian converted to the proper way of making green tea."

Richard glanced at the wall clock.

"Well, I better get going. You probably have work to do, and I have a workout in the afternoon."

"*Torture*, you wanted to say."

"I'm sorry, *torture*," he emphasized the word and looked at her with a spark of humor in his eyes.

He stood up and motioned in the direction of the bedroom.

"Let me say goodbye to Lucky," he said.

They went to the bedroom where Lucky just opened his eyes and yawned. Richard squatted near the dog and scratched the dog's ears. Laura leaned on the doorframe with crossed arms. It never ceased to amaze her to see how gentle Richard's touch was when he petted Lucky.

"See you sometime in the future, buddy. Get well and listen to your boss."

Laura walked Richard to the front door.

“Laura, would you like to go on a dinner with me?” She heard slight nervousness in his voice. His question startled her.

“When?”

“On Saturday?”

“I… This weekend won’t work for me. I have a backlog of work. I hope you understand.”

“Sure, no worries. Well, see you and Lucky in the woods, I guess.”

He turned around and strode to his car.

“Richard…” Laura whispered.

He backed up his car and drove away. She stood on the front porch and looked at the car disappearing in the distance. Things were back to normal. But was that what she really wanted?

Chapter 6

"The wounds are scabbed over. I would still be careful with him for another week or so, though," Chris said.

"Can I start taking him for short walks to the woods or is it still too early?" Laura asked.

"Short walks will be fine. No running, though. Keep him on the leash and walk slowly."

"Of course. I'm just sad to see him walking around the house. He needs some fresh air."

"That's understandable. He's an outdoor dog. You can also let him walk in the backyard. Just don't let him get too vigorous with his exercise."

"Definitely. Thank you, Chris."

"You're welcome. Lucky should be fully recovered in a week or two. But if you see anything worrying, as always give me a call. If everything's okay, there's no need for another check-up."

Laura left the clinic and guided Lucky to the car. It filled her heart with sadness to see him limping on the pavement. She reminded herself that in a few weeks he would be jumping and running around her as usual.

Laura pulled into the driveway and closed the gate. She let Lucky loose to walk around the backyard. They would go on a short walk to the woods in the evening.

She went inside, made herself some green tea and opened the front door to let Lucky in. She plodded to the bedroom with Lucky limping behind her. She turned on the laptop and checked her email. Three new gigs, deadline for tomorrow. Just what she needed right now when she just wanted to fill her bathtub with hot water and read a good book.

She opened her word processor and started working on the outlines of the three new articles due tomorrow. She typed on the keyboard with reluctance, her slow moving hands reminding her of a zombie from a TV show she watched last night. The work had never felt more gruesome to her.

Three hours and three thousand and fifty five words later, Laura closed her laptop and went outside. She sat in the chair overlooking a small garden with some shrubs and flowering plants whose names she could never remember.

She hadn't seen Richard since their last meeting on Thursday. Everything should feel normal to her, but it didn't. She realized she hadn't talked to anyone except for Chris for a good five days. She grabbed her cell phone and called Samantha.

"Hey, Samantha."

"Hi, Laura. How are you?"

"I'm fine, thanks. Listen, Samantha, are you free now? Would you like to grab some tea and sit in the garden with me?"

"Let me finish this chapter and I'm all yours. Six is fine?"

"Sure. See you."

She hung up and looked at the garden. Laura had always wanted to have a small vegetable garden in the backyard, but never got around to it. She decided she would take care of it tomorrow.

***

"So, when will Lucky be able to play with Winston again?"

Samantha and Laura were sitting in the wooden garden chairs in the backyard of Laura's house. Lucky lay on a green plaid wool blanket between the chairs.

"Chris said give or take two weeks and he'll be fully recovered."

"That's great news. Winston will be happy to hear that. When I take him for a walk, he's always looking around as if searching for Lucky."

Laura smiled and sipped her tea.

"Hey, how's Richard?"

"What about him?"

"Haven't you met with him today?"

"No. Why would I?"

"To help you with Lucky?"

"Lucky can walk. I no longer need Richard."

"What about your... *acquaintance*?"

"What about it? I told you he was just helping me out. I no longer need his help so he's out of my life," Laura said, her tone a bit angrier than she wanted it to be.

"Laura, I can tell you're angry. What's going on?"

"Nothing. I... I just liked talking with him. He asked me if I would go on a dinner with him and I said no. He left and we haven't talked ever since."

"Why did you say no?"

"Because I'm confused. I like him, but I don't want to get involved."

"Get involved in what?"

"Samantha, he's different than the guys I've just slept with. He makes me feel like I'm talking with an old friend. And it scares me."

"So there's something more than just this 'helping out' aspect?"

"I feel attracted to him. I think he feels the same way about me. But at the same time I enjoy being single."

"At some point casual stops satisfying you, doesn't it?"

"I… I guess you're right."

"Why don't you call him and ask him if he still wants to go to dinner with you?"

"No, that's out of the question. I'm not going to make a move on him."

"What are you going to do, then? Keep sweeping your garden and coming up with other things to occupy your mind? You think I haven't noticed? You never pay attention to your garden."

"Samantha, I just want to talk. You speak to me like a psychologist."

"I'm sorry, you're right. How do you feel about it, then?"

"I feel confused. The last time I had tea with him, it felt *right*. It felt as if that's how my day should look."

"Are you afraid of changing things up?"

"Changing things how?"

"I mean, being single is like your identity. You've been single your entire adult life. You're afraid you'll lose a part of your personality, aren't you?"

"I… I think so. I need independence. Nobody tells me what to do."

"But on the other hand you feel there's something missing in your life."

"I hadn't felt it before I met him, for God's sake. I regret I let him help me with Lucky."

"What's done is done. The question is what you're going to do now."

"Let's change the topic. How's your new book coming along?" Laura asked.

"It's going pretty well. I'm well ahead my schedule."

Samantha's cell phone interrupted their conversation.

"Hey, Chris, what's up?" Samantha said. "Oh, you didn't have to do that. Listen, I'm at Laura's place now. If you keep it in the oven, it will stay warm for another thirty minutes or so. I'll be back by then."

She paused to listen to Chris.

"Perfect. See you in thirty minutes, honey."

Samantha hung up.

"Listen, Laura. Chris cooked something special. I left a note saying I would be back at seven thirty. It's almost seven already."

"It's okay, I understand."

Samantha finished her cup of tea. She crouched beside Lucky and stroked him.

"See you, Lucky. Get well. You'll play with Winston soon."

When Lucky heard his best friend's name, he opened his eyes and raised his head.

"Not now, buddy. In a week or two," Laura said. She smiled when the dog tilted his head sideways as if asking if she was serious.

Laura walked Samantha to her car.

"Thank you for coming," Laura said.

"No problem. If you want to talk about anything, call me."

Samantha got inside her car. Laura waved goodbye and stood on the driveway until the car disappeared around the corner. She went inside and grabbed Lucky's leash from the wooden coat hook near the door.

She took Lucky on a leash and went to the forest. The dog had been sleeping almost entire day. A short walk would do him good. It would also do her good, if they meet Richard.

Laura walked the main trails in the forest for ten minutes when she saw somebody jogging in the distance behind the trees. She stopped on the trail and hoped Richard would see them and say hello. She didn't want to strain Lucky.

The person in the distance took a left turn behind the trees and appeared on the main trail. To Laura's sadness, it wasn't Richard. She turned around and walked back home. Lucky limped behind her, happy to be back in the forest. At least the dog was pleased.

They arrived at home ten minutes later. Lucky went to sleep right after they got inside. No wonder, the dog almost hadn't left her home for the last week. He had been still recovering. It would probably take at least a few weeks before he would be back to his normal stamina.

Laura sat at the beige couch in the green-painted living room and stared at the TV set. If it was a normal day, she would grab some popcorn and watch a movie or two. Today, it felt pointless to her.

She went to the bathroom and filled the bathtub with hot water. She removed her jeans and a white top. Then she took off her black panties and bra and entered the bathtub.

The hot water relaxed her muscles. She reached for a bottle of bath salts. A soothing fragrance of lavender filled the air.

It smelled like Richard's soap.

Chapter 7

"Hey Lucky. Why are you barking?" Laura was on her knees in the garden planting peas in a raised garden bed, which she read would make it easier to tend the plants. Two similar beds stood behind her.

"Hey Laura." She turned around and saw Richard looking at her. The sun illuminated his face and made him look like an angel. His fitted white shirt and khaki pants only helped with the illusion.

"Hi, Richard." She tried hard not to jump from joy after seeing his face for the first time in two weeks.

"I was just passing through. I thought I would check on you, see how Lucky is doing. I can see he's pretty healthy."

Lucky trotted to Richard. To Laura's relief, Lucky's wounds had healed completely. He walked with no visible limp, as if the last two weeks had been just a bad dream.

He crouched to pet Lucky. The dog lunged at him and put him off balance. Richard lay sprawled on the grass while Lucky stood over him and licked his face.

Laura burst out laughing. Lucky was a large dog, but he was no match to a man of Richard's size. He found a weakness in the man and took advantage of it. The dog wagged his tail like a helicopter.

"Oh God, you could be a little bit less emotional, brother," Richard said with a wide smile on his face. He surely enjoyed the warm welcome, even if he tried to act with composure. He propped himself on his arms and rose up.

"How are you doing, Laura?" he said dusting off his shirt.

"I'm fine. I've been busy with the garden," she pointed to the garden with raised beds and fresh soil.

"I see. What's that over there?" he pointed to a bed in the back of the garden.

"Broccoli."

"And this one here?"

"Lettuce."

"What were you planting when I interrupted you?"

"Peas."

They stood in awkward silence. His attempts at small talk made Laura uncomfortable.

"So, what you've been up to? I haven't seen you jogging in the last week."

"I had a minor injury and had to take a break from running."

"Are you okay now?"

"Yeah. It was just a strained ankle. You need to stay off your feet for a few days and you're good to go."

"Listen, Richard. I was about to take Lucky for a walk. Would you like to join us?"

"I… Sure, why not."

"Let me change my clothes. I'll be back in a jiffy," she said and left him in the backyard with Lucky.

Five minutes later, they left Laura's house and turned left to head to the forest. Lucky walked in front of them, pulling Laura on the leash.

"What about your decision?" Laura asked.

"Decision about what?"

"Getting a dog."

"Ah. I decided to put it on the back burner. I don't want to make an emotional decision."

"That's a good approach."

"I can always stop by and take a walk with you and Lucky, right?" he joked.

"Feel free to join us whenever you want. Just give me a call," she said in a serious tone, much to his surprise. The last thing she wanted was to get Lucky used to Richard. At the same time, though, she wanted to see Richard more often.

"Sure. Thank you," he said with a light note of astonishment in his voice.

They entered the forest and walked down a narrow trail through the trees. Lucky was no longer limping, but Laura was afraid to let him loose. She figured it was better to wait for another week or two before she would let him wander again.

"How's your job?" Laura asked, trying to avoid another awkward silence.

"It's going really good, thank you. Clients are getting leaner and stronger. One of my trainees is almost ready for a competition next month."

"So you also coach people for competitions?"

"You wanted to ask if my job exclusively entails torturing poor people who want to lose some weight? The answer is no. I have a few trainees who don't think of me as their oppressor."

"Very funny."

Richard sent her a playful smile. Laura couldn't feign her anger when she looked at his amused face and exuberant eyes. She smiled back.

"By the way, I made green tea your way," Richard said.

"You did?"

"Well, I didn't follow it to a tee. I don't have a tea thermometer. But I waited for a few minutes after the water boiled. It had to be around seventy five degrees."

"Three minutes of brewing?"

"Three minutes. Measured with a stopwatch in hand."

"Good. How did it turn out?"

"Not as perfectly as yours, but it was still much better than what I used to drink. It's funny I've been doing it the wrong way my entire life."

Laura pondered the last two weeks and thought how happy she was to talk with Richard again. She started to think she had also been doing it wrong her entire life.

"You live and learn," she said, more to herself than to Richard.

"Absolutely."

Lucky barked and pulled Laura on the leash to the right. His powerful pull snatched the leash from her hand. She tripped over a root and was about to fall when Richard grabbed her from the back. A squirrel ran away a few yards from them and climbed up an acorn tree.

Richard stood behind Laura, his muscular arms on her waist. She felt a warm feeling spreading from her tummy in all directions. His hands felt so right on her belly, as if they were created to hold her narrow waist. She felt Richard's breath on her neck and waited for him to kiss her.

"You okay?" Richard asked with concern.

"I… I'm okay, I guess."

Lucky stood under the tree and barked at the squirrel watching him from up above.

Richard let Laura go and crouched in front of her.

"Better check it. Lift your foot and move it in a circle," he said with a concerned voice.

She followed his orders without any questions.

"Is it painful?" he asked.

"No."

"Put it down, please. And sit on this trunk right there," he said and pointed to a tree trunk right beside her.

He removed her shoe and pulled down her sock. Laura was glad she had painted her nails cherry red in the morning.

His gentle and warm touch felt more sensual to her than every foot massage she had ever received in her life. And Richard was just inspecting her ligaments, checking if she hadn't twisted her ankle.

She jerked her foot away.

"What's wrong? Was it painful?"

"No. You tickled me," she said and chuckled.

He smiled and put on her sock and shoe.

"I think you're good to go. You were lucky. It's easy to twist an ankle this way."

"Thank you, Richard." She hoped her voice didn't sound dreamy.

"You're welcome. We shouldn't press your luck any further today. Let me walk Lucky."

"All right."

Richard walked to Lucky, who stood under the tree and watched the squirrel. Laura was surprised the dog paid no attention to them when Richard inspected his ankle. Lucky had always been protective of her. Well, he must have figured out Richard hadn't been a danger.

Richard grabbed the leash lying on the moss covered forest ground.

"Let's go, buddy. No more chasing after squirrels," he said.

Laura rose from the trunk and joined them on the trail.

"Do you want to walk back home?" Richard asked.

"No, I feel okay, really. Let's make our usual circle."

They followed the trail among the trees. Lucky walked right beside Richard's foot. Give him two weeks and the dog might as well move in with him.

"So that's your usual walk with Lucky, huh?" Richard asked.

"We have a few different trails. Since I don't want to strain him too much, today we took one of the shortest."

"I usually jog here in the morning."

"In the morning? What about evenings?"

"Sometimes I jog twice a day. A quick jog in the morning, a proper one in the evening. Depends on my shift."

"Don't you, like, ever get tired?"

He laughed. "The more you exercise, the more energy you have. Up to a point, of course. I know my body enough not to cross it."

"Any other activities? Gym, running, rescuing careless women from tripping over roots. What else?"

"Biking, swimming, tennis with Chris from time to time."

"Excuse me, are you a human being or a machine?"

"I need to be a shining example for my clients. Including the ones I torture." He sent her a wink.

They turned right on the trail leading back to town. The afternoon sun shone through the canopy and illuminated their path. She looked at Richard who had just turned his head to Lucky. The dog gazed back at him with a happy look on his face. Laura saw warm camaraderie between them. If someone saved your life, you're bound to get close to him pretty quickly.

"When Lucky gets better, you should try jogging with him. You take long walks, anyway. Why not help him get back into shape sooner?" Richard asked.

"Me and jogging? No way."

"I forgot. Jogging and torture are synonyms in your dictionary."

"Right on."

"I'd love to teach you how to run properly. But hey, it's your call."

Was she just imagining things or had he just teased her?

"You? Teach me?"

"Why not? I run regularly, anyway. You could join me tomorrow in the morning."

"Would we have to run fifty miles or whatever your usual light session is?"

"Sixty miles will be fine."

"Thanks, but no thanks."

"Fifty? It will be fun, I promise."

"Nope."

They left the narrow forest trail and entered the main trail. Laura could see the edge of the forest in the distance.

"At what hour do you run?"

"Seven."

"Have I heard you right? Did you just say eight?"

"Exactly, eight."

"Eight it is."

He stopped in his tracks and sent her a questioning look.

"Are you serious? I was just kidding. I respect your preferences."

"Hey, you've been wrong your entire life about making green tea. Maybe I'm wrong about running."

"So you really want to go on a run with me tomorrow?"

"I do."

"Perfect. Wear comfortable sneakers. Something similar to the ones you're wearing now would be fine."

"Alrighty, boss. Anything else?" She sent him a flirtatious look.

"Shorts and a top would be fine. It's going to be hot tomorrow," he said.

Laura was more than sure of that.

Chapter 8

Laura had never thought that learning how to run could be so sexy.

She stood on the trail with Richard, who had been focused on fixing her posture. He was dressed in simple black running shorts and a white sleeveless shirt. It was the first time she could see his massive shoulders and arms without a piece of clothing covering them.

"Head high, back straight," he said.

"Back straight," he repeated and touched her back. "Just like that."

"What about my head?"

"It's okay. Just focus your gaze about forty yards in front of you."

"Like that?" she asked.

Richard touched her chin and tilted it upward. His hand touching her jaw made her legs wobbly. She imagined him pressing her against the tree.

"Laura? Pay attention," he said in his professional teaching voice and looked straight into her eyes.

"What about my legs?" she asked to break the tension and take her mind off her naughty thoughts.

"We'll come to legs later. Now, your shoulders. When you run, keep them relaxed and parallel to the ground."

"Okay."

"If you feel your shoulders tensing up during the run, shake them out like that," he said and showed her how to do it.

"Shake them out. Got it."

"Now, your arms and hands. Cup your hands."

Laura cupped her hands.

"Not so loose. Imagine you're holding an egg. Good."

Richard kept explaining to her how to maintain a proper running form. Laura didn't pay much attention to it. She followed his orders as best as she could, but her focus was on his touch. His hands touching her jaw, waist, legs, back. Running had its appeal. She had definitely been wrong about it her entire life. She could run every single day – as long as Richard was there with his reassuring touch to make sure she had the perfect form.

"Now that we've covered all bases, we will walk for one to three minutes and run for one minute. No talking until we're done. I don't want you to lose your breath."

She was tempted to say she had already lost her breath when he touched her this way. "Okay," she said instead.

They walked for about three minutes in silence. Then Richard patted her on the lower back and started running. She followed him as best as she could.

"Good. Keep your arms a little higher. And remember – back straight," he said after a minute of running.

They repeated the same pattern for five more rounds, shortening the walking break from three minutes to one minute. Laura was surprised she didn't feel exhausted. In fact, she felt exhilarated. She doubted it was because of running, though.

"Good. Really good. Did you really have your last jogging session three years ago?" Richard asked. They sat at the bench near the edge of the forest.

"At least three years ago. Except for my one-off visit in the gym, I haven't had any other exercise except for long walks with Lucky."

"That explains why you're so fit. Most people can't catch their breath after the workout we did today."

"Seriously?"

"I'm serious. But then again, I can tell by your body these long walks do you good."

Had he just complimented her?

"Thanks," she replied, unsure what else to say.

"Anyway, good work today. Same time tomorrow?" he said and rose up.

"Sure." She didn't want to go home yet, but didn't know how to let him stay for a while longer.

"Have a great day, Laura."

"You too," she said, unhappy to see him go.

***

"Keep your back straight. Remember, when you slouch, you can injure yourself pretty bad," Richard said.

Laura slouched only because her legs felt tired after their third consecutive day of running, but she didn't want to show him she was weak. She was an independent and strong thirty-five-year old woman, after all.

"Okay, okay," she said and hyperextended her back. Richard sent her a threatening stare.

"Just kidding," she said and fixed her posture.

"One more run and we're done for today. Ready?"

"As ready as always."

In fact, she was dead on her feet. Except for when Richard touched her to correct her form, running had lost its appeal. It was again just what it had been to her before she tried it – a torture. Walking breaks were under a minute. Most of the time they ran, and faster than the day before, at that. She felt as if there were hundreds of little spikes piercing her legs.

They began to run again. Laura turned her head away from Richard to hide her scowl. She was done with running forever.

When they finally finished and reached the bench, Laura had to fight the temptation to lie down on the bench. Instead, she sat down and bowed her head down to hide her long breaths beneath her long hair.

"How was it for you today?" Richard asked.

"It was okay," she said and sent him a quick smile.

"Laura, if it gets too difficult for you, just tell me."

"I said I'm okay."

"I'm sorry, I didn't mean it that way."

His concerned voice made her feel ashamed of her uncontrolled burst of anger.

"I'm sorry. I'm just a little tired," she said and turned her head to look him in the eye. The concern in his eyes made her even more ashamed of shouting at him.

She leaned her face into his and looked into his eyes. Their faces were only inches apart. She looked at his full lips and stubble on his chin. He swept her blonde hair to the side. His fingers brushed her right ear.

Laura closed her eyes in anticipation and begged him in her mind to kiss her already. She felt his warm lips brushing the corners of her mouth. Then he gave her a light kiss. It sent a jolt throughout her body. She opened her mouth and let him slide his tongue inside. Their tongues caressed each other. She slid her hand down his muscular chest and felt warmth spreading through her entire body. Richard pulled his face away and smiled.

"Did you want to say something?" he said.

"I'm sorry I yelled at you."

"How sorry are you?"

"Very sorry," she said and leaned her face into his again. They kissed for what felt like forever to her. Long, wet, passionate kisses from Richard sent her over the moon. She wanted him to undress her right there and caress her entire body with his muscular, yet gentle hands.

"I think it's enough exercise for today," Richard said. "Someone's coming."

Laura pulled her face away and moved away from him to keep up appearances. A large gray dog ran toward them. A woman with chestnut hair followed.

"Hey, Winston," Laura said. Samantha's gray Irish Wolfhound, who was a beast of a dog almost half of the size of an adult, jumped at Laura with joy and sent a questioning look toward Richard.

"It's okay Winston, Richard is cool," she said. The dog left her and sniffed Richard. Richard extended his hand and let the dog sniff it.

"Are we cool, buddy?" Richard asked.

The dog wagged its tail and lay down its head on Richard's lap.

"I guess we're cool, then," Richard said and stroked the dog's head.

Samantha approached them.

"Hi, Samantha," Laura said in unison with Richard. Wow, that felt awkward.

"Hey, Laura. Hi, Richard. What you're up to?" Samantha said.

Laura and Richard. Laura liked the sound of it.

"Richard is teaching me how to run."

"You? Running?" Samantha chuckled.

"She's making fast progress," Richard said.

"That's surprising considering that she has always hated running."

"Hello? I'm here listening to you," Laura said.

"Well, it's never too late to shake things up. Isn't it, Laura?" Samantha said and winked.

Laura sent her a threatening look.

"Winston, I see you've found yourself a new friend," Samantha said.

The dog turned around to gaze at her and switched his attention back to Richard.

"You're such a traitor," Samantha said.

Laura chuckled. It wasn't only Lucky that was charmed by Richard. It seemed the man could charm every dog in the world.

"Well, I better get going. I want to get back before Chris is awake. See you later, Laura."

"See you. Have a good one."

"You too. Bye, Richard."

Richard waved to Laura and patted Winston goodbye.

"We were almost caught. By my best friend, at that," Laura whispered to Richard.

"Almost is the key word here," he said and smiled.

She gazed at his lips, eager to get another taste.

"Laura, would you like to go to dinner with me?"

"I…" She hesitated for a moment, thinking of the last time he asked her the same question and how afraid she was to get involved. "I would love to. Absolutely."

Richard smiled from ear to ear.

"Would Saturday work for you? Six o'clock in the evening?"

"Sure. Where do you want to go?"

"That's a surprise."

“Okay.”

They rose up from the bench together and walked in silence to the edge of the forest.

“See you on Saturday, then,” Richard said and gave her a light kiss.

“See you, Richard. Thank you for the… exercise today.”

“You’re welcome.”

He gave her a quick hug and walked away.

Laura walked home with dreamy eyes. Her legs no longer hurt.

Chapter 9

"Is it too tight?" Richard asked.

"No, it's okay," Laura replied. Richard touched the blindfold once again to make sure it wouldn't slide off her eyes.

"We're good to go," he said and gave her a peck on the lips. He turned the engine on and backed out of the driveway to her home.

"Aren't you going to tell me anything about where we're going?"

"Nope."

"How stupid do I look with this blindfold?"

"You look adorable."

"What if someone sees me?"

"It's getting dark. Besides, who cares? Let adults have some fun."

Laura was surprised to discover yet another side of Richard she hadn't even suspected existed. She didn't expect him to be so carefree.

"Sit back and relax. We'll be there in about fifteen minutes," he said.

Twenty minutes later, Richard stopped the car.

"Okay, we're here."

"Can I take it off now?"

"Just a second. You'll take it off inside."

"Are you serious?"

"Yep. I'm the boss tonight. Come with me."

Richard took her arm and led her twenty steps or so. She heard the door open. Richard put a hand on her lower back and guided her inside. She heard faint instrumental Japanese music and quiet conversations around them.

"Take off your shoes," he said.

"What?"

"Just please take off your shoes."

She removed her high heels and felt smooth wooden panels under her feet.

"What do I do with them?" she asked.

"Give them to me."

She heard him putting her shoes on a wooden pad or something with a similar sound.

"Now what?"

"Come with me," he said and took her hand. She enjoyed the feel of his strong hand holding her tiny hand.

He led her through the room for thirty steps or so.

"Now we sit. I'll help you," he said.

Laura squeezed his hand and sat down. She was glad she didn't wear a shorter skirt.

Richard let loose of her hand.

"Now we can take it off." She felt his fingers untying the knot of the blindfold.

"Ready?" he asked.

"Ready."

Richard took off her blindfold. Light from a lamp hanging above them blinded her for a moment as her eyes adjusted to the brightness.

They were sitting in front of a low dark brown wooden table. On the table there was a glass vase with white flowers and bamboo placemats.

Laura realized they were in a traditional Japanese restaurant. She had no idea how Richard found this place, as she had never heard of a Japanese restaurant in Maple Hills.

"Are we in Maple Hills?" she asked.

"Nope. Oak Valley. It's a new place. They opened last week."

She nodded and turned around. Their table was separated from the next table by a thick dark brown wooden wall. The beige-painted walls were empty except for a few drawings here and there. Laura chuckled when she noticed other people sitting in the restaurant. They had to see her in a blindfold being led by Richard to their table.

A woman dressed in traditional Japanese clothing approached their table and handed them menus. The names of the dishes were written both in English and Japanese.

"*Sukiyaki. Tempora. Tonkatsu.* How am I supposed to choose anything from it? The only dish I recognize is sushi."

"Don't worry. I have no idea either. Let's ask the waitress."

Richard called the waitress. She appeared a few seconds later. They asked her about the most recommended dishes. Laura chose Korokke Soba, a deep-fried dish related to the croquette with buckwheat noodles. Richard ordered shabu-shabu, thinly sliced beef boiled in water and served with tofu and vegetables.

"Now the best part," Richard said.

The waitress came back with another menu. Laura opened it and realized it was a menu dedicated to teas.

Laura felt like a kid in a candy store. "There must be at least fifty different kinds of tea here," she said.

"That's why I wanted to take you here. I heard about it from a friend who was here last week and mentioned a wide selection of teas."

"A wide selection? Richard, this is crazy. You can even order matcha tea."

"I have no idea what that is, but I guess it means something good."

"I've always wanted to try it, but never had the opportunity."

"Now's the time," he said and smiled.

They ordered tea they would drink before their meals would be ready. Laura chose matcha tea, while Richard ordered rice-scented Pu-erh tea.

Five minutes later, the waitress brought two traditional black iron Japanese kettles with two matching cups in the same design. She put one kettle and cup for Laura and another kettle and cup for Richard.

"Oh my God. It's delicious," Laura said after she took a sip of her tea.

Richard smiled.

"How's yours?" she asked.

"It's… interesting. The scent is a little overpowering. I guess you can get used to it. Wanna try?"

"Sure."

Richard poured the tea from his kettle into Laura's cup.

"That's… bad. Really bad." She wrinkled her noise. "Try this," she said and poured Richard her tea. He sipped the tea in silence.

"So, how is it?" she asked.

"You're right. It's really bad after trying your tea. But hey, you're the tea expert here, after all."

Laura sent him a playful smile. She hadn't had the chance to get a good look of Richard when he picked her up and told her to wear a blindfold. Now she could get a better look while they waited.

He was dressed in a navy jacket, fitted blue shirt and a burgundy tie. He didn't even forget about small details – his dark gray socks worked well with his medium gray pants. In this outfit, he looked more like a fashion stylist than a personal trainer.

She liked his attention to detail. Most men she met with were sloppy dressers. But then again, they didn't take her to a Japanese restaurant and she usually only saw them once or twice.

"If you like it so much, you can buy it here," Richard said.

"The tea?"

"Just ask the waitress. They sell them by weight."

Laura called the waitress and bought an ounce of the tea.

Two minutes later, the waitress came back with a tray of food for Laura and a minute later for Richard.

When they finished their meals, it was already nine o'clock.

Laura loved every little part of their dinner. She liked the goofiness of Richard blindfolding her for the trip. It was sexy when he casually brushed her knee on their way to the restaurant. Her senses were heightened and his casual touch felt like a sensitive massage.

She liked how thoughtful he had been to remember her love for tea and take her to a paradise for tea lovers. And the food. She still felt the incredible taste in her mouth. She could eat there every single day.

"I don't think I have ever eaten something as delicious as what I just ate."

"Likewise."

They paid their bill and left the restaurant. Richard, a gentleman as always, opened the door for her.

"Will you blindfold me on the way back?" she asked.

"Do you want me to?"

"I liked it, but I can do without it. I want to know the route to this incredible place."

Richard turned the engine on and left the parking lot of the restaurant. Laura turned around to remember how the entrance looked. It had wooden panels and Japanese signs. Nobody would mistake it for something other than a Japanese restaurant. She shifted her attention back to the road and Richard.

"I loved the dinner, Richard. Everything was perfect."

"I'm glad to hear that." She could hear a hint of delight in his voice.

Fifteen minutes later, they passed the "Welcome to Maple Hills" sign.

"Would you like to get another cup or two of matcha tea? You didn't have the chance to really taste it at the restaurant because of your tea. I felt bad for you when I saw you drink it," Laura said and chuckled.

"Very funny. It wasn't that bad. And I never leave food unfinished. Tea included," he said. "As for your idea… Why not? Let's go to my place. It's closer."

He turned right at the intersection and drove into the neighborhood Laura had visited the last time when Lucky was gone. She shuddered.

"Everything okay?"

"Sure. I just remembered the last time I was here. Following your car and dying of stress because of Lucky."

"I remember. You were pretty rattled, to say the least."

He pulled into the driveway and turned the engine off. He left the car and circled it to open the door for her. She could get used to this treatment.

They entered Richard's home. The last time she had been there, the only thing she had on her mind was Lucky. She didn't have an opportunity to look around, except for the bedroom. The main hallway was painted in a shade of green. The kitchen was at the left, the living room was at the right and the bedroom was at the end of the hallway in front of them.

Richard led her to the kitchen. It had a minimalist design. She was surprised how clean it was and how few things there were on the countertops. It was the total opposite of her kitchen.

"I didn't expect your kitchen to be so… organized."

"What did you expect from a machine?"

He sent her a playful look. She liked this side of him more and more.

"Right. I forgot."

"All right, let's make the tea."

Richard pulled out a tea thermometer and an egg timer from a drawer.

"What's that?" she asked.

"What's what? Proper equipment for the perfect tea, my lady. Has nobody told you how important the temperature and brewing time are?"

Laura burst out laughing.

When they made the tea, Richard guided her to the spacious room across the kitchen. They sat on a plush beige sofa in the middle of the room. It seemed Richard liked the minimalist style.

The cream-painted living room had a sofa, a small dark brown coffee table on which they put their mugs, two armchairs of the same type as the sofa, a TV set, and a single bookshelf. There was also a small standing lamp in the corner of the room that Richard turned on instead of the main lights.

Richard sat close to Laura and put his right hand around her waist. They sat in silence and sipped the tea.

"So, are you done with running forever?" Richard asked.

"Why do you say that?"

"I saw your look during our last session. I've been coaching enough people to recognize what it meant."

"Guilty as charged."

"I think there's potential in you. You have much more stamina than most people. The first days are always the hardest, even if the first day is easy."

"I'll think about it."

"You better do. Running with a partner is more fun than running solo."

"Like I could keep up with you for fifty miles."

"Step by step and you'll reach it."

"Right."

"Regarding our last exercise…"

He leaned his face into hers and gave her a gentle kiss. He looked into her eyes, as if looking for permission to kiss her again. She placed her hand on the back of his head and pulled him closer.

"This one?" she whispered and kissed him on the lips. He bowed his head to kiss her neck. She felt a light bite that sent a tingling sensation through her body. His lips traced her neck. He kissed her below the earlobe and left a warm trail of kisses all the way down her collarbone. Then he returned to her lips. His warm tongue entered her mouth. Heat spread throughout her body. She let out a light moan.

He unbuttoned the first three buttons of her shirt and slid it off her right shoulder.

"This one," he said and nipped her collarbone.

Laura had no control over her body. His every touch made her shiver with desire. She removed his jacket and tie and threw them across the room. Then she unbuttoned his shirt and traced his chest with her palm. The firm muscles of his chest and abdomen felt like a smooth rock. He wasn't a machine. He was a piece of art. A perfect sculpture.

Richard unbuttoned the remaining buttons of her shirt and threw it over the coffee table right beside their mugs with cooling tea. Laura removed his shirt as he unhooked her bra.

"And this one, too," he said and slid his tongue across her nipple. She was burning with desire and craved his touch all over her body. Nobody had ever made her feel this way, including her best short-term lovers. There was something else in the way he touched her. It wasn't only about his touch. His mere presence made her elated.

She scratched her nails down his back and pressed his face into her breasts. She felt his warm tongue circling around her nipples and sucking on them. Laura arched her back and threw her head back with a moan when she saw a framed picture on the bookshelf. The living room was dimly lit, but she could still make out the features of a female face she had already seen. The face of a woman from a photo on the nightstand in Richard's bedroom.

She pulled his face away.

"Richard. Please stop. I can't."

He sent her a questioning look. Hot desire burned in his dark eyes.

"I… I have to get going."

"Laura. What is going on?"

"Nothing. I… I just have to get going." She reached over for her bra and put it on.

"Why? What happened?"

"I need to take Lucky for a walk."

"Now?"

"It's almost eleven. I took him for our last walk over six hours ago."

Richard looked at her with a startled expression as she rose up and buttoned her shirt.

"At least let me drive you home."

"No, I'll manage."

"I insist."

"Thank you for the dinner, Richard. It was fantastic. But now I have to go. Alone."

She left the room in the hurry, walked down the hallway, opened the door and left Richard's home.

"Laura, please wait," he said.

She didn't turn around. Neither did she answer his calls when he called her twice a few minutes later.

Chapter 10

"And that's when I realized he isn't serious about me. I mean, how can you get involved with someone and still keep framed photos of your deceased wife all over your house?" Laura said to Samantha.

They sat in Laura's backyard and sipped the matcha tea Laura bought the day before in the restaurant. She wore sunglasses to hide her reddened eyes after a sleepless night of crying. Lucky slept on a blanket in a shaded area of the garden.

"I can imagine it was pretty devastating to notice it in such a moment," Samantha said.

"Don't even remind me of it."

"You need to talk with him."

"Talk about what? There's nothing to talk about."

"Talk about his wife. Ask him how he feels about you."

"It's pretty obvious. He's just looking for some fun, while I no longer can think of him this way. You know how it always has been for me with men."

"Are you sure he's just looking for fun?"

"Wouldn't he get rid of the photos of his deceased wife if he was serious?"

"Laura, is this only about the photos or something else? I think you're not telling me something."

"She looked pretty similar to me. For all I know, he might have thought yesterday he was kissing his wife, not me."

"So that's what it's all about?"

"I just realized I don't want to let go of control in my life. He's making my life so complicated."

"Maybe it's just a coincidence you look alike. Maybe he likes blond women. It doesn't already mean he's looking for someone to remind him of his wife."

"Maybe, maybe, maybe. Samantha, I'm done with maybes. I shook things up, and it didn't work. Single life is easier. Nobody can hurt you. You're in total control."

"Laura, I'm just trying to help."

"Fine. I appreciate it. But now, let's just enjoy the sunshine. How do you like the tea?"

***

When Samantha was gone, Laura went back home to lose herself in the work. She checked her email. No new messages. No new gigs. Perfect. When she needed the work, she didn't have it.

She went back to the garden and picked a shovel. It was time to plant some new vegetables.

She worked like a horse the entire afternoon in the blazing hot July sun. Out of habit, she reached into the pocket for her cell phone. She reminded herself she left it inside so she wouldn't hear Richard's calls.

When she was done planting beans, she headed to the garage to leave the shovel and other gardening tools. She opened the door of the garage and left the tools at the end of the room. When she turned around to leave the garage and close the door, she noticed Richard standing in the driveway.

"Hi, Laura."

She stood silent.

"Can we talk?"

"I can't. I'm busy." She closed the garage door and began walking to the front door of her house.

Richard took her by the arm. "Please. Just a minute."

"What do you want?"

"What is wrong? Why did you go yesterday?"

"I just had to go."

"Then why won't you return my phone calls?"

"I left the phone in the house. I was working in the garden."

"What about my phone calls yesterday?"

"I..."

"Laura, what is wrong?"

"Richard, please leave me alone. I enjoyed our running lessons and the dinner, but it has to stop."

"Did I say something wrong? Was what happened yesterday too soon to you?"

"No."

"Then what is wrong? Can you tell me what is wrong?"

"I thought you were seeing me because you like me and you like spending time with me."

"That's exactly why I'm seeing you."

"Listen, Richard. I saw the photos of your wife at your home."

"And?"

"And I think we have different feelings."

"Different how?"

"She looked pretty similar to me."

"She did. But I still don't understand it."

"Richard, are you seeing me because I remind you of your deceased wife?"

"I'm sorry?"

"Do I mean something to you or am I simply reminding you of your wife?"

"Are you implying that I thought you could replace Olivia just because you also have blond hair and blue eyes? Did you think I was looking for a *replacement*?"

"I…"

"Seriously?"

"No, it's just that…"

"You know what. You're right. We're done."

Richard turned on his feet and stormed off.

Chapter 11

"Hey, Tim," Laura said to the phone.

"Hi, babe. Long time no see. What's up?" Tim replied.

"Wanna see me?"

"Today?"

"I'm free at eight."

"Works for me."

"See you at eight, then."

"Sure thing, babe."

Laura was glad to see Richard go, but she was sorry their conversation had to end that way. Perhaps she had been too harsh, but it didn't matter now. She was free from Richard, back to her safe single life where she was the only person responsible for her happiness.

She went back home to doll herself up for Tim's visit in the evening. She had to remind herself how good it felt to share company with someone with no strings attached. Besides, it would help her forget about Richard and regain control over her life.

She took a shower and put on makeup. Then she slipped into her nicest black set of lingerie and a tight fitting red dress. Laura was ready to rediscover the perks of single life.

She heard the doorbell rang.

"Hi, babe. Gorgeous as always," Tim said. He wore a simple black t-shirt and blue jeans that were a size too big for him. Dressing sharp wasn't his strength, but he was pretty good in bed. Besides, Laura had a thing for brunets with a military haircut.

"Hi, Tim." She motioned him to get in. "Anything to drink?"

"Wine would be fine."

"I have Chardonnay and Sauvignon blanc."

"Chardonnay would be perfect. Thanks."

She led him to the kitchen where she poured wine for both of them. Lucky entered the kitchen to inspect the stranger. He approached him, sniffed his leg and left the kitchen, as if his companionship was below his standards. She heard him lie down in the living room.

Laura guided Tim to the bedroom. She closed the door and sat beside him on the bed. Tim put his hand on her lap and slid it across her thigh. He put his glass of wine on the nightstand and took hers from her hand. They started kissing.

To Laura's horror, she started fantasizing about Richard's lips kissing hers. Tim wasn't a bad kisser, but he didn't take his time like Richard did. She scolded herself for thinking about him and switched her attention back to Tim. She removed Tim's t-shirt and let him slide down her dress. She pushed him on the bed to straddle him.

"So sexy," Tim said as he admired her in lingerie. Laura felt his hands reaching around her and unhooking her bra. He threw it away and squeezed her breasts.

"You like it when I touch you this way, don't you?" he said.

"I do." She enjoyed the last time he bossed her around in the bed. Now, she only felt emptiness, as if all they did was just crossing tasks off a step-by-step list to a few seconds of meaningless ecstasy.

When she looked at his face, she realized he had been more concerned about her breasts than herself. Not that it wasn't the same when she slept with him a few weeks ago. This time, though, it bugged her so much she put his hands away and rose up from the bed to look for her bra.

"What are you doing?"

"I'm no longer in the mood."

"You're what? First you call me out of the blue, now you're saying you're not in the mood?"

"Tim, just please get dressed and go."

"Seriously? I said no to another chick just to be with you tonight and now you're brushing me off."

"That's so touching. Thank you. I really appreciate what you did for me. Now go."

He rose up from the bed and put his t-shirt on. Laura didn't bother to slide into her dress again. She was going to slip into something more comfortable and watch TV. They walked down the hallway. She opened the door for him.

Richard was on the doorstep and was about to ring the doorbell.

"What the hell? Don't ever call me again, bitch," Tim said. He sent Richard a threatening look and stalked out of her house. "You're ugly, anyway."

"Richard, what are you doing here?" Laura asked. She realized she was only in her lingerie.

"The better question would be to ask what you are doing."

"I..."

"I thought I was too harsh on you and wanted to talk things over again. But I guess we're really done."

He turned around and left her standing on the doorstep. A tear streamed down her face as she stood in lingerie and watched him leave her driveway. Forever.

Chapter 12

"Richard, please talk with me."

Laura stood on Richard's porch and banged on his door. She knew he was home. His car was in the driveway and she had already asked at the gym when his shift ended.

"Go away," she heard his muffled voice behind the door.

"Richard, please. We need to talk."

"There's no longer anything to talk about. Go back to your boyfriend."

"He's not my boyfriend."

"So you're giving out your body to a total stranger? Perfect."

"Richard, it's not like that."

"I don't care."

"Can you open the door so that we can talk like adults?"

"No. Leave." She heard him walking away from the door. Laura turned around and went back home.

***

Laura spent the entire afternoon in bed mulling over what happened in the last three days. Lucky lay with her, though he didn't offer her a lot of consolation. He reminded her of Richard. Richard and his gentle hands caressing Lucky's head.

She was mad at herself for being so impulsive when she had seen the picture of Richard's wife. What did she know about being a widower, anyway? Why did she expect him to hide the pictures as if his wife had never existed?

And what was that with Tim? Did she really think she could erase her memories with Richard by sleeping with a random guy?

It was too much for her. She had no idea what to do. Laura realized there were some things she can't deal with by herself. She reached for her phone.

"Samantha. Can you come?"

"Laura, what happened?"

"Just please come."

"I'll be there in fifteen minutes."

***

"And that's how it all ended," Laura said as she finished recounting what happened between her and Richard since she had last seen Samantha.

Laura sat huddled with Lucky on the bed. Samantha sat across Laura in a chair she brought from the kitchen.

"Samantha, do you think it can be fixed?"

"I… I don't know." Samantha usually had great ideas, but this time she appeared to Laura as confused as she was.

"I only realized how much he meant to me when I lost him. How ironic is that?"

"Have I told you how I met Chris?"

"You did."

"Do you remember the story with Victoria? I was ready to pack my things and leave town."

"I remember."

"Things worked out well in the end. Ironically, I think the whole situation only strengthened our bond and made us both realize how much we meant to each other."

"Richard hates my guts."

"He does now. Doesn't mean he will when you give him some time to think about it."

"I can't think straight. Me, such an independent woman. I can't shake it off and move on."

"When you get involved, you can't just shake things off like that, Laura. But time heals all wounds."

Laura felt as if her wounds would never heal. There was an empty place in her heart, and nobody would fill it but Richard.

When Samantha left her house, Laura went to the bathroom and filled the bathtub with hot water. She removed her pajamas and got into the bathtub. She reached for her favorite bath salts. She sobbed as the aroma of lavender filled the air. The aroma of Richard's soap.

***

Two weeks had passed. Richard didn't pay her a visit. Laura gave up on calling him and visiting him at the house or at the gym. She walked around her home in a mindless state. She was late with her work and left her home only to take a walk with Lucky. Samantha called her a few times, but she told her she wanted to be alone.

She was making coffee when she noticed a jar of matcha tea standing in the corner. Her hands trembled and she dropped a glass carafe with coffee. The glass exploded into hundreds of little pieces all over the kitchen. A large puddle of coffee streamed down the white-beige tiles.

Laura yelled in anger and stormed off the kitchen. She changed into shorts and a t-shirt, put on sneakers, closed the door to her house with a bang and broke into a sprint.

Running at full speed with tears streaming down her face, she reached the edge of the forest in a little over a minute. She came to a halt to regain her breath. Two minutes later, she broke into a light jog. She was going to run until her legs gave out.

She ran across the trail she had walked with Richard when she took Lucky for a walk. She ran across the trails where they'd had their running sessions. She passed the place where Richard had found Lucky. She went deeper and deeper into the heart of the forest to the places she had never reached. The trail got narrower and narrower.

Birds chirped around her. Her hard steps echoed through the air. She heard rustling to her right and turned her head to inspect the source of noise. As she saw a squirrel climbing a pine tree, she hit something with her right foot and found herself flying face first into the ground.

The last thing she felt before the world went black was a piercing burning pain in her lower leg.

Chapter 13

She opened her eyes and saw Richard's terrified face above her. He was saying something to her, but she couldn't make out the words. Burning pain seeped through her right leg. The world went black.

When she regained consciousness, Richard was carrying her through the woods. She heard his heavy breathing as he took long steps through the forest. She closed her eyes to stop her head from spinning.

She heard the siren of the ambulance in the distance. She realized they were at the edge of the forest, because she could no longer see the canopy above her head.

Laura lay in an ambulance. A paramedic was checking her vitals. She had a throbbing headache and felt like throwing up. "We're taking you to the hospital," she heard the paramedic say.

***

Laura woke up in a hospital room. The harshness of the light blinded her for a moment. Someone held her hand. She saw Richard's relieved face above her.

"Hello," he said.

"What happened?"

"You tripped over a stone. You had a concussion and you fractured your tibia. You also had symptoms of sunstroke."

"Where's Lucky?"

"Samantha is taking care of him."

"Good." Her throat was sore. She had difficulty speaking.

Richard helped her drink a cup of water.

"What did I tell you about taking things easy?" he said.

"Sorry, Coach," she said and sent him a weak smile.

"You were lucky I took a long run. I usually don't run that far away. The doctor said you could have died there." His voice cracked. "How did you even get there?"

"I just ran."

"You just ran. I found you ten miles away from the town."

She raised her head and looked him in the eyes. He had dark circles under his eyes. She realized he had been with her the entire time.

"How long was I out?"

"About twelve hours. It's five in the morning."

"Richard, I'm so sorry."

"Let's not talk about it now. You should rest."

"Richard, I have never met someone like you."

"Laura, please. Get some sleep. We will talk about it when you get better."

"Could you please stay with me and hold my hand?"

"I will."

Laura closed her eyes. Sleep claimed her seconds later.

***

"My sweet boy," Laura exclaimed as she entered her home two days later. Richard held her left arm to help her keep balance as the dog jumped at her with joy.

"Enough, buddy. Let your mommy sit down," Richard said and guided her to the living room.

Laura had to walk with a crutch. The doctor said she would have to walk with it for at least two weeks. She was lucky she only had a minor fracture of her tibia.

"Matcha tea?" Richard asked.

"Yes, please." She could drink it now that she was back with Richard.

He disappeared in the kitchen while she sat at the sofa and petted Lucky. The dog kept wagging his tail and jumping with joy.

Richard returned a few minutes later with a kettle, two cups of tea, the tea thermometer and an egg timer. She watched him make the tea the way she had taught him. He handed her a teacup.

"I forgot how delicious it was," she said.

"I noticed it was almost full. Why haven't you drunk it?"

"I… I couldn't drink it. It reminded me of you."

"Laura…"

"Let me speak first. I'm terribly sorry what happened between us. I overreacted. I shouldn't have been so harsh about the pictures."

"You were right about them. I have to move on."

"Still, I shouldn't have been so… impulsive. Do you forgive me?"

"I forgive you. But you were still right. I gave you the wrong impression."

"About this man at the doorstep… Nothing happened between us. I thought he would help me forget about you. But I couldn't stop thinking about you."

"Laura, let bygones be bygones."

"I still want to explain myself. Look, Richard, I've been single my entire life. I have never had a real relationship with someone I cared about. I had to be independent," she said and looked him in the eyes. "I needed to control everything. I couldn't control my reaction when I saw the photo of your wife. It freaked me out."

"But when I lost you, I realized I made a mistake," she continued. "I realized I was afraid of getting involved because I didn't want to get attached. Attachment was the total opposite of independence for me."

Richard began to say something when she placed two fingers on his lips.

"Now I understand I only robbed myself of the most beautiful thing in life. When I saw your face in the woods after the accident, I thought I was in heaven." She chuckled.

"Laura, I was so scared when I found you there. There was a pool of blood under your leg. You had a cut on your forehead."

"At least I had the privilege of being carried by you," she said to ease the atmosphere.

"I shouldn't have been so angry at you for so long. We could have talked it over sooner."

"You had your reasons."

"I drew conclusions too soon. Laura, I need to ask you the same question. Do you forgive me?"

"I forgive you. We both made mistakes."

He embraced her. She felt safe in his strong, muscular arms.

"Richard, do you remember when you joked you weren't getting a dog because you could always see Lucky?"

"I do. What about it?"

"Would you like to see him more often?"

"What do you mean?"

"Would you like to move in? Lucky would be so happy to have you every single day."

"Lucky, you say?"

"Okay, okay. *I* will be so happy to have you every single day."

"I would love to. No offense to Lucky, but I would move in only because of you."

He leaned his face down to kiss her. She felt his warm lips on hers. A familiar warm feeling spread throughout her body.

"I think I forgot something from the bedroom. Could you help me get there?"

"As you wish, boss." He put his hands under her back and legs. He carried her to the bedroom and laid her on the bed.

"And please close the door. We won't need Lucky for a while longer."

Chapter 14

"Where do you want me to move the bookshelf, honey?" Richard asked.

Laura pointed to the corner of the room. "You can put it in this corner."

She liked the look of their new living room. Lucky liked it, too. He had been accompanying them when they had been moving furniture, up to the moment he found a quiet corner behind the sofa and fell asleep there.

"Richard, I'm so happy you moved in," she said when he was done moving the bookshelf.

"I'm happy, too. Now I have unlimited access to Lucky." He sent her a playful look.

Lucky woke up as if on command when he heard his name. He trotted over to Richard and demanded petting.

"Yeah, we're talking about you, brother," Richard said and patted the dog on the head. Lucky wagged his tail in a circular motion and licked Richard's hand. He couldn't get enough of him.

Laura couldn't, either. She walked over to them and embraced Richard. He smelled of lavender soap. Lucky walked around them as they kissed, unhappy that he lost their attention.

"I love you," Richard said.

"I love you, too."

He held her in a firm embrace that made her feel that everything in the world was right as long as Richard was with her. She looked into his eyes and saw a drop of sweat on his forehead.

"Break?" she asked.

"Would be nice. I think I moved more furniture today than in my entire life."

"Would you like some green tea?" Laura asked.

"Absolutely. Seventy five degrees, three minutes."

A Dog’s Life

Chapter 1

Ashley was glad she had a day off. She was tired of her grumpy manager, Courtney, who treated everyone like a stupid child needing her expert advice with everything. If you made a mistake, Courtney was always there to scold you. She would never miss the opportunity to make you feel bad. But the job paid Ashley's bills. Well, at least some of them.

On her days off, Ashley looked for new freelance jobs online. Web design sucked, too, but at least there was no cranky boss above her. She could also work at her own pace. She sat at her laptop and recorded video applications for new gigs.

Smile, say a few words about yourself, tell the potential employer how professional you are and how much experience you have. Post your application and hope it will be noticed among thirty other people.

As much as she hated using her looks to get a job, there was no other way to stand out among East Asian workers willing to work for five bucks per hour. A video application featuring a beautiful ginger with long thick hair, full lips, hazel eyes and light freckles often did the trick, as long as her application was even read.

Her Irish Setter, Violet, nudged her. Ashley glanced at the wall clock. It was three o'clock, time for a walk with Violet. She turned her laptop off, leashed her dog and went outside.

Her walks with Violet were one of the highlights of her daily routine. She was glad she lived so close to the woods. As boring and quiet as the town was, she could never live in a concrete jungle. Maple Hills was, is, and would always be, her home.

She walked down the stone driveway of her house and turned right. Mrs. Smith was walking her beagle on the other side of the street. Ashley waved to her and kept walking down the sidewalk.

She could see pine trees about half a mile in front of her. They marked the entrance to the forest, one of the reasons she loved the town so much. You could enter the woods and keep walking for hours without meeting other people. Not that she hated other people. It was just nice to escape it all and spend some time with only her thoughts. Well, with Violet, too. You could trust dogs. Unlike people, as she learned from Spencer.

She passed the houses of her neighbors. Mr. Walker mowed the lawn, Mrs. Gomez read a newspaper on her porch. Just another lazy Sunday in the town.

The entrance to the forest was right across the street. Ashley let Violet loose. Nobody drove through this street on Sunday. Heck, nobody drove through this street on most days. Violet broke into a trot and hurried in front of her. Ashley was about to cross the street when she heard the sound of a loud engine coming from her left. A black Cadillac Escalade sped down the street.

"Violet!" she yelled.

Violet stood in the middle of the street, confused by a rare sighting of a car on the road that had been empty nearly any other time. There was little traffic in the town. Violet had never learned that cars could be dangerous.

Ashley ran out onto the street and waved to the driver to stop. He was either blind or drunk. Violet stood right in the middle of the street and he hadn't already stopped.

"Stop! Stop!" Ashley shouted.

She tensed her muscles for the incoming hit. The car broke to a halt a feet away from Ashley and Violet.

"What the hell was that?" Ashley yelled to the driver.

A thirty-something blond man in an expensive gray suit jumped out of the car. A businessman type, probably a prick who thought he was the most important person in the world.

"I'm so sorry," he said. His voice was shaken and his eyes were wide in shock.

"You almost hit her," she said through gritted teeth. Without Violet, her world would fall to pieces.

"I'm so terribly sorry. It was my fault."

"It damn well was your fault. What the hell are you, blind?"

"My GPS stopped working. I took my eyes off the road for just a few seconds."

"Said every driver after the crash. Why the hell are you even driving down this road? Nobody uses it."

"My GPS got it all mixed up. I'm so terribly sorry. Do you want me to drive you to a vet, check if everything is okay with your dog?"

"You didn't hit her, but you were damn close."

"I'm really sorry." The driver almost begged her to forgive him. His hands were still shaking. At least he felt guilty.

Violet walked over to the guy and sniffed him. To Ashley's surprise, she wagged her tail. The driver stroked her head.

"It's okay," she said. Violet hadn't been hit, and that was the most important thing. Now Ashley just wanted to get rid of the guy.

"If you need anything, I mean, anything, please call me. I'm terribly sorry for what happened." He handed her a business card. She glanced at it and put it in her pocket.

He walked back to his car and drove away.

Ashley crossed the street and entered the forest. She pulled the card from her pocket. "Matt Hansen," it read. "Blue Oak Technologies, CEO." She crumpled it in her fist and threw it into the trash can.

Chapter 2

"Hi, sis. Good to see you," Julia said.

Ashley and her older sister sat in Julia's office at the gas station. Julia was only two years older than Ashley, but she had already been the owner of a profitable gas station, as profitable as a gas station in a small town could be.

"Hi, Julia. First things first…" Ashley pulled a wad of money from her pocket. "One, two, three, four, five." She counted the one hundred dollar bills and put them on the table.

"Ashley, you don't need to count it."

"Just making sure I took the entire amount. Thank you so much again, Julia. You saved my life last month."

"No worries. Is business better this month?"

Business. As if her freelancing gigs here and there could be called a business.

"It's getting better. At least enough to pay all my bills this month."

"I'm glad to hear that."

"How's your day?"

"Busy as always, but you're just in time for my break. How's your day?"

"Besides almost being ran over with Violet by a six thousand pound tank, it's okay."

"A what?"

"I took Violet on our usual walk at three o'clock. Right beside the entrance of the forest a guy almost ran us over."

"On Pine Street? I thought it was closed."

"It isn't closed, just not in use."

"What happened?

"A black Cadillac appeared out of nowhere. Violet stood in the middle of the street, apparently fascinated by the prospect of being ran over by such a nice car."

"You should teach her that cars are dangerous. I think I told you that how many times… Five hundred?"

"And how am I supposed to do it? Get run over by a car in front of her and hope she'll figure out I'm in pain?"

"I don't know. Ask a dog trainer or something."

"Sure. Anyway, this guy jumps out of his car, shaking like a leaf and telling me his GPS stopped working. He said he took eyes off the road for just a few seconds."

"Every driver says something like that after a crash."

"That's what I told him. But then Violet walked over to him and wagged her tail."

"Seriously? I always thought she was more reserved toward men than you are."

"Very funny."

"Just kidding. What happened next?"

"This guy, he stroked her head and she just stood there, happy, as if nothing happened."

"Are you sure she's all right? Maybe you should take her to a dog psychologist or something."

"I was thinking about it."

"So, you stand in the middle of the road and a guy is petting your dog. A dog who's afraid of strangers. Then what?"

"Then he gave me his business card and hit the road."

"A business card? What for?

"He said if I needed something, I can call him."

"How fast did you throw it out? The second he gave it to you?"

Ashley chuckled. She loved how well her sister had known her.

"A minute later."

"Did you even read it?"

"I did."

"What did it say? What a guy in such an expensive car would do here?"

"Mitch Hansel or something. CEO of something with Technologies in the name. Probably just passing through."

"Wait, wait. Hansel, you say? Not Hansen?"

"Maybe Hansen."

"Sis, you had the pleasure of being the first person in town to welcome Mr. Hansen as a neighbor. Well, the first after Rachel Ross. He bought the house through her."

"He did what?"

"Matt Hansen is our new neighbor. Rachel told me a rich guy is moving into town. It had to be him. Now that I think about it, I recall she told me he was driving a black SUV."

"Oh my God. You cannot be serious."

There was a knock on the door.

"Come in," Julia said. Ashley always admired how imperious her sister's voice got when she spoke to her employees. They knew she was the boss.

A twenty-something tiny blonde girl Ashley has never seen around at the station entered the office.

"Mrs. Pine, there's a problem with a customer. Could you help us out?" She was practically begging Julia.

"I'll be there in a second," Julia said. "I'm sorry," she said to her sister.

"It's okay. I was just leaving, anyway," Ashley said.

They rose from the chairs and walked together out of the office. Ashley was always amused by the attention they got from other people when she walked with her sister side by side. If it wasn't for Julia's shorter hair and her fondness for high heels, they would be a spitting image of each other.

"See you around, sis," Julia said.

"See you. And thanks for the money again."

"No problem. Be on the lookout for our new neighbor. Maybe welcome him with a cake?" she chuckled.

"Shut up."

Chapter 3

It was beyond Ashley's understanding how Spencer could dare to show up at her door again and beg her to get back with him.

Did he really believe she would forgive him for what he had done? What was she supposed to say? It's okay you screwed my colleague in the car right in front of me. It's really fine. I'd like to be with you again because you're such a nice faithful man who makes my life so great.

Someone tapped her on the shoulder.

"Ashley? There's a guest at the table over there. What are you doing?"

Ashley turned around. Her manager, Courtney, with a trademark scowl on her face, pushed her to serve the guest.

"Right there. Are you blind?" Courtney pointed to a table in the far corner of the room that had been empty a few moments ago.

She glanced in the direction. Mitch or whatever his name was sat at the table waiting for the waitress.

"Courtney, I need to go to the bathroom. Can somebody else serve him?"

"No." Courtney was helpful and understanding as always.

Ashley plodded to his table.

"Hello, sir. Can I help you?"

"Yes, I'd like…" He raised his head to look at her. "Oh, hello."

Why did he have to remember her face?

Her only escape was to keep a professional attitude and get away from him as soon as possible.

"Would you like a starter, sir?"

"No, thank you. Just a main course."

"What would you like for a main course?"

"Spaghetti alla carbonara, please."

"Would you like anything to drink?"

"Yes, I'd like a cup of orange juice, please."

So far, so good. She walked over to the kitchen and ordered his dinner. She served him his OJ and walked back behind the counter. Spencer had disturbed her, and now this guy again. She glanced at her watch and realized her shift wouldn't be over for another three hours. She exhaled a long breath and tapped her fingers on the counter.

"Ashley, carbonara is ready."

"I'm sorry, Jim."

She took the tray from the kitchen and walked over to Mr. CEO. The door to the restaurant opened and Spencer entered the room. He looked at her with a careless smile on his face. What a jerk. What the hell was he doing there? Did she need to get a restraining order against him to free herself of his presence? Stalking was a good enough reason to get a restraining order, wasn't it?

She felt something slipping from her hands. There was a splashing sound and the loud sound of the metal tray hitting the wooden floor.

The crisp white shirt of Mr. Important was covered in spaghetti and sauce. He had a baffled look on his face. The food slipped down his pants. The rest of the spaghetti was on the floor, along with the metal tray.

Ashley gazed with bewilderment at the tray of food. There was silence in the room. All guests stopped eating and watched the scene.

Courtney stormed out of her office. "Ashley, what the hell have you just done?"

"It wasn't her fault. She was about to put the food on the table when I reached for my cup of juice," the rich guy said. She didn't remember him reaching for juice. Had he just lied for her?

"Ashley, explain yourself," Courtney said.

"I..."

"She is one of the nicest waitresses I've ever had the pleasure of being served by. Please don't punish her for something she hasn't done. As I said, it was my fault. I'm not angry."

"Ashley, why the hell are you standing here like that? Bring Mr. Hansen a towel to clean his shirt." Courtney said. "I'm very sorry, Mr. Hansen. I hope it won't affect your opinion of our establishment, sir."

Ashley rushed to the supply room for towels. She managed to hear Mr. Hansen saying that as long as such nice waitresses worked there, he would keep coming for dinner.

She took a pad of paper towels with shaking hands and returned to the table. She gave them to Mr. Hansen, who sent her a wink. What was that? Was there a spark of amusement in his eyes?

"The meal is on house, Ashley," Courtney said. "Go and order it again."

She reordered the food and returned behind the counter. Spencer sat in the middle of the room. She thanked God Kate was at his table. Ashley was tempted to go to his table and yell at him for putting her off balance. But she knew it wouldn't be a good idea. Courtney was already pissed off enough, and if Ashley stepped on her toes again, she would for sure be fired. As crappy as it was, she couldn't afford losing this job. Yet.

When Mr. Hansen was done with his meal, she approached his table. She took a glance at his shirt. It was ruined, there was no doubt about it.

"Can I bring you anything else?"

“No, thank you.

Ashley started to walk away when she realized she had forgotten something.

“Thank you for defending me. Why did you lie for me?” Ashley whispered. She glanced at the left and saw Spencer looking at them.

“It was the least I could do to make amends for almost running over your dog. In fact, you should have done it a few times more. I would definitely feel a little less guilty.”

She couldn’t resist a chuckle. She didn’t expect Mr. CEO to be so good-natured. Hell, he was quite *okay*, and okay was one of the words she thought she would never use when describing any male.

“Thank you, Mr. Hansen.”

“Matt. Matt is fine, Miss…?”

“Ashley. Just Ashley.” She heard someone open the door of the office.

“Thank you for your service. It was excellent,” Matt said in a loud voice.

Courtney approached the table.

“Was everything to your satisfaction, Mr. Hansen?”

“Most certainly.” He pulled out his wallet.

“Mr. Hansen, the meal is on the house,” Courtney said.

“I’d like to give a tip to this wonderful waitress. What is your name, Miss?”

“Ashley.”

“A tip for Ashley, one of the friendliest waitresses I’ve ever had the pleasure of being served by.”

He put a twenty dollar bill on the table, grabbed his jacket and left the restaurant.

Courtney exchanged a bewildered look with Ashley.

"You? Friendly?" Courtney said. "You're lucky he was so understanding. I would have fired your ass if it was your fault."

She left the table. Ashley put the bill in her pocket and walked over to the counter. She avoided looking at Spencer. Better not encourage him to talk with her again or she was sure to break something and lose the job. And this time nobody would defend her.

Chapter 4

Three hours later, when her shift was finally over, Ashley headed home. She leashed Violet and went to the forest. There were still at least two hours of light left, enough for a longer walk to get her thoughts together.

She walked beside towering pine trees and young acorn trees peppered between the evergreens. The woods were her escape. The trails close to the edge of the forest were often frequented by fellow dog owners, but when you got deeper into the woods, you were usually alone. It was a perfect place to collect your thoughts and calm yourself down, especially with your faithful dog walking right beside you.

Violet trotted beside Ashley. Her paws rustled the grass that grew on the sides of the narrow trail leading deep into the heart of the forest where all the beaten paths ended. The path was getting narrower and narrower, swallowing Ashley into the welcoming forest. She had never felt like a stranger there. Quite the contrary – the forest was her ally, her escape from the town and all the people who could make her so angry.

She heard footsteps coming from her right. As far as she knew, there was no trail parallel to the one she followed. Nobody would walk across the dense forest, unless it wasn't a person, but an animal. She grabbed Violet by the collar and stopped.

The footsteps were getting closer and closer. No, it had to be a human. But who would traverse the woods in July? There were no mushrooms to pick. She heard another set of footsteps. A smaller creature. A dog?

Something black showed through the trees and shrubs. Something beige and brown followed it. Someone walking a dog?

Violet withdrew behind her. Ashley had read that Irish Setters were great hunting dogs, but Violet was anything but a hunter.

A man dressed in a black t-shirt and khaki pants emerged from the woods. He looked familiar to Ashley, but she couldn't place who it was.

Then she realized it was Matt Hansen. He looked so strange because it was the first time she saw him in casual clothes. Besides, he would be the last person she would expect so deep in the woods. And the dog. There was a dog walking beside him, probably a mutt. If she were to guess, a bit of a German shepherd with a mix of Golden Retriever. It looked familiar to her.

"Hel–" He came to a stop. A wide smile, as if someone surprised him with a birthday party, appeared on his face. "Oh, hello, Ashley."

"What are you doing so deep in the forest?"

"I could ask you the same question."

"I asked first."

"I took a walk with my buddy Duke." The dog sat beside Matt and looked at Violet with a terrified gaze. So far it seemed that Matt somehow hadn't noticed Ashley's dog yet.

"Duke? Is it your dog?"

Now she knew why the dog looked familiar. It was Duke from the animal shelter where she had been volunteering in her free time. It was so strange to see him walking on a leash with Matt, a dog that had lived in the shelter for the last year, that she couldn't believe it was really Duke.

"Since Tuesday. I adopted him from the shelter. Now, what about you? Why are you walking alone so deep in the woods?" he said.

"Not alone." She pointed to the dog that hid behind her with such a skill that Matt didn't notice her. "I walk here every single day with Violet."

"Oh, hello to you," he said.

To Ashley's surprise, Violet came out of her hiding place behind Ashley's knees. She approached Matt and jumped at him with a wagging tail. It seemed she really liked him. When Duke saw Violet approach Matt, he withdrew a few steps.

"Now that we're talking..." Ashley pulled out a twenty dollar bill from her pocket. "I can't accept it. Thank you for defending me at the restaurant, but this is too much."

"It's okay. I really enjoyed your service."

"Please. It convinced Courtney I was supposedly the best waitress in the world, but I can't accept it." She extended her hand. "I insist."

"All right." He took the bill from her.

"Now, what's the story with Duke? I help James and Melinda at the shelter. I know him," she crouched and extended her hand. "Duke, buddy."

Duke looked at her. There was a glint of recognition in his eyes, but he was afraid to approach her because of Violet. Duke had always been a timid dog. It was a surprising choice for a man like Matt.

"I went to the shelter, saw him and adopted him," he said.

"And that's it? Why Duke? Nobody has even wanted to see him before with him being an old dog and all."

"I figured that puppies will always be taken by somebody. An old dog like Duke? No chance. Besides, I like his character."

"His shyness?"

"No, there's much more to him. There's potential for a great dog. I just need to help him forget about his past."

Forget about his past? Was the rich guy really so nice or did he have a secret agenda? Had he somehow found out she volunteered at the shelter?

"Why don't we take a walk together?" Matt asked.

"Okay," she said. She wanted to be alone, but he had saved her skin at the restaurant. It was the least she could do.

Ashley let Violet loose, while Matt kept Duke leashed. The trail was so narrow that they had to walk in a single file. Violet led the way, Ashley followed her, behind her was Matt and Duke walked on the man's right side.

"You still haven't told me why you were walking across the forest instead of following a trail," she said.

"If I told you, you wouldn't believe me."

"Try me."

"I was looking for food."

"You were what?"

"I told you that you wouldn't believe me."

"Why were you looking for food? In the woods?"

"It's my hobby. I'm a survivalist."

Survivalist. Ashley had read an article about them. They were the crazy people who kept tons of food and firearms in their cellars, ready for the world to end. He might not have been a jerk, but he was definitely a little bit crazy.

"And what does it have to do with walking across the dense forest?"

"I like to know what resources are around me." He pulled something from his right pocket and opened his palm. "See, there's food here. Wild blueberries."

"I… I never knew there was anything edible in these woods." She was embarrassed she had been living in the same town for thirty four years and didn't know there were edible berries in the forest.

"It's just one of the things I found here." He pulled something from his left pocket. "Here's another." He held a couple of leaves.

"Mint?" she asked.

"Peppermint to be exact."

"Ew." She grimaced. Ashley had hated peppermint ever since her sister had made her try peppermint tea.

"Not a fan, I presume?"

"I don't have fond memories of mint. Did you find anything else?"

"I ate some wild raspberries. There's also stinging nettle. I think I also saw some Jerusalem artichokes. And you can always eat the inner bark of a pine tree." He pointed to pine trees on both sides of the road.

"How long have you been walking across the forest?"

"An hour or so."

Ashley was embarrassed. He had barely moved in and knew more interesting things about the forest than she did. No more talking about the woods. She had to change the topic.

"How do you like the town?" she asked.

"I love it. It's perfect. Just what I needed."

"So was it a permanent move or just a temporary thing to recharge your batteries?"

"A permanent one. I'm done with big city living."

"Are you looking for a job here?" The conversation was turning into an interrogation, but she was curious why a businessman type would move to Maple Hills. It was a town where you were one of the most successful people if you were an owner of a small gas station.

"No. I'm retired."

Retired? Had she heard him right? He couldn't be older than forty, and maybe even much younger than that.

"Retired?"

"I sold shares in my company to my partners and left it. I no longer enjoyed the work."

"I see."

She hoped there was no envy in her voice. She would love to be able to leave the job at the restaurant and do something else with her life.

"Let's turn right here. The path is wider," she said. She was tired of turning her head around to talk with Matt.

"What about you? I've been going to the restaurant every single day since I've moved in. Today was the first time I saw you there."

"It's a part-time job. I also do some freelancing stuff here and there."

"Freelancing as in what?"

"Just some boring stuff."

"Tell me."

Ashley was confused. Had she really heard sincere interest in his voice? She hadn't noticed anything of the usual stuff guys did to pick her up. Just genuine interest.

"Web design. Websites, logos, and stuff."

"Good for you."

"Yeah." Ashley hoped he would get her message and change the topic. She wasn't passionate about her work.

"Hey, Duke, let's go over here," Matt said. The dog pulled on his leash in the direction of an acorn tree standing in the middle of the pine trees right beside the trail. Ashley saw a squirrel climbing the tree.

To Ashley's surprise, the dog turned around and trotted over to Matt. Duke had never been a particularly obedient dog at the shelter.

"Are you a dog trainer? Duke has never been an obedient one."

"I have no experience with dogs. I guess he's just glad I took him from the shelter."

"Could be."

"Speaking of the shelter… you said you work there?"

"I help James and Melinda whenever I can. It's just a volunteering job."

"You three are doing a splendid job there. I've always thought that animal shelters look like prisons."

"Most shelters do. Maple Hills' one is different."

"It sure is. And James and Melinda are some of the nicest people I've ever met."

Ashley smiled. The shelter felt like second home to her.

"It's a shame the budget is tight, though. We would love to build more shelters and repair the old ones," she said.

"James and Melinda told me about it. It's a sad situation, indeed."

There was real concern in his voice. Perhaps she had really judged him wrong. Her sister was quite rich, after all, and she was anything but a jerk.

They walked for a minute in silence. Ashley saw an opening in front of them. They would walk out on the street on the other side of the town.

"Where are you heading?" Matt asked.

"To the left."

"I'm heading to the right. Thanks for the walk, Ashley. It was nice to meet you."

"Likewise."

Matt turned right and left her standing at the edge of the forest. Ashley turned left to head home.

She didn't lie. To her surprise, she did enjoy taking a walk with Matt. He wasn't a jerk, after all. He was quite a nice guy.

Chapter 5

"Ashley, you will never believe what has just happened," Melinda said in an excited voice. "I wanted to call you, but since you told me you'd come today, I figured it would be better to tell you in person."

Melinda had always been a cheery person, but this time she was giddy like a teenager. She waited for Ashley at the gate instead of welcoming her at the office. It was funny to see a fifty-seven year old woman with strands of gray hair acting like that.

"What happened?" Ashley asked. They walked together to the office where Ashley would change into working clothes.

"Twenty thousand dollars."

"I'm sorry?"

"Twenty thousand dollars. Somebody sent us a check for twenty thousand dollars."

Ashley stopped in her tracks.

"Are you serious?" she asked.

"Serious as a heart attack."

"Oh my God. That has to the best thing I've heard this year." She jumped from joy. The news had made her day.

"Ashley, we will finally fix the old houses and even build a couple new ones," Melinda said.

"And there would be still a lot left for food," Ashley said.

"And we can finally get a better refrigerator."

"Melinda, who sent it? Is it somebody from the town?"

"It's an anonymous donor. Sent from a Delaware-based company."

"You can check the records online."

“I looked it up. It’s private data. Anyway, don't look a gift horse in the mouth, right?” Melinda smiled and patted Ashley on her back. “Let’s get to work. There’s a lot to do.”

“As always,” Ashley said. And as always, she looked forward to it.

Three hours later, after feeding twenty dogs and cleaning three kennels, she took a break to drink some coffee with Melinda and James, her husband.

When James and Melinda Brooke sat together on the old sofa with a red plaid blanket on top of it, they looked more like siblings than a couple. Both were tall and lanky. If Melinda hadn’t dyed her hair black, they would look even more alike.

“Any new adoptions recently?” Ashley asked.

She sat in her usual place, an armchair with a green plaid blanket on top of it. With all the old furniture, the place looked like a cabin in the woods. Ashley wouldn’t change a thing in there.

“A beagle puppy yesterday. Buster on Thursday. And two mutt puppies from the Millers’ on Wednesday,” Melinda said.

“Nice. So many good news.”

“And there was also Duke on Tuesday,” James added.

Ashley put a cup of her coffee on the table and feigned surprise. “Duke?” she asked. She didn’t want them to know she had known Matt.

“This new guy adopted him. He didn’t even want to look at the puppies. He said, ‘Show me the dogs that have been here the longest,’” James said.

“And he took Duke just like that? No objection from Duke?”

“You should have been here to see this. Duke actually *jumped* at him with joy. Wagging tail and all that,” he said.

“You’re kidding, right?”

"I was there with them. Never in a million years would I have thought Duke could be so welcoming," Melinda said.

"There's always a first time for everything. I'm glad he found a new home," Ashley said.

"And the guy was really nice. What was his name, Mark, Mike?" Melinda said to James.

"Matt," he said.

"Right, Matt. A really nice fellow. Asked us a lot of questions about the shelter."

"And you should have seen his car. Black Cadillac Escalade, the newest model. He must be rich," James said.

James eyes went dreamy when he spoke about the car. He had to be a huge fan of Cadillacs. Ashley hadn't known this side of James. Besides, she had always spent much more time with Melinda.

"As if she cares," Melinda nudged him.

"We better get to work. There's still a lot to do," she said and stood up.

"Could you clean Duke's kennel first? We will have some new puppies on Monday. I want to put them there," James said.

"Sure."

Ashley left the office. She headed left to the kennel that was right beside the wooden fence of the horse riding school. The school also belonged to James and Melinda. Ashley had never cared much for horses, but she respected James' and Melinda's work. The school provided a lot of fun to some kids and adults, too.

She reached the last kennel and opened the door. Each kennel in the shelter was actually a small wooden house, not a regular shelter you would buy for a dog sleeping in the backyard. Ashley had always joked with Melinda that if they would ever run out of cash, they could clean up the kennels and open a small hotel. Most kennels weren't much bigger than a walk-in closet, but a single bed would still fit there.

Ashley swept the floor of the kennel expecting Duke to come back from his walk at any moment. Then she realized that Duke had no longer lived at the shelter. He had a new home and a new owner.

A new owner. Matt. Retired entrepreneur. Rich person, capable of donating to worthy causes. Or to show off.

Ashley threw the broom across the room when she remembered what she had told him about the shelter the day before.

Chapter 6

"Julia, you need to help me," Ashley said.

She walked to the gas station just after the closing hours to catch Julia before she headed home. Ashley stood near the door of her sister's office. Julia packed her handbag.

"What about the Brookes'?" Julia asked.

"I already asked them. They don't know anything except for the fact he lives in a large house."

"What do I tell Rachel? 'Hey, sorry for calling you on Saturday evening, but could you tell me real quick the exact address of the last home you sold in Maple Hills?'"

"That could work."

"You shouldn't have thrown away his business card."

"How was I supposed to know I would need to talk with him? He was just a guy who was passing through the town."

"Why do you even want to talk with him, anyway?"

"I've already told you. I can't tell."

"I would love to help you, but I can't. Rachel wouldn't tell me."

"Could you at least try, please?"

"Listen, Ashley. This is confidential data. She can't just tell anyone whose house she has sold recently. It's illegal."

"Okay, I'm sorry. You're right."

"But maybe this would help you out… Richard told me that Matt is his new trainee. I think he works daily with him in the evenings. Maybe you'll catch him at the gym."

"Thank you, sis. That's helpful. I'll check it out." She spun on her heels and started walking toward the door. "Oh, and sorry for stealing your family time."

"No worries. We're family, too. If it's anything important about Matt, please tell me. I'm always there if you need me."

Ashley walked to Julia and hugged her. "Thank you," she said.

The Maple Hills Gym was located just a few minutes away from the gas station. It was one of the newest buildings in town. The building's facade was covered in glass, so Ashley could see the people who worked out on the equipment located close to the front.

She saw Richard, one of the gym's personal trainers who had also been Julia's friend. He spotted for Matt, who was doing bench presses.

Ashley opened the glass door and entered the gym. Matt had just finished his exercise and headed to the locker room. Richard had been already gone. At least she wouldn't have to wait.

"Stop," Ashley said in a forceful voice. There were a couple more people in the gym, but she hadn't even glanced their way.

"Hello, Ashley." He sent her a smile, as if everything was all right.

"Do you really think it would impress me?"

"I'm sorry. What would impress you?"

"The donation. You hear me say I love the shelter, so you shell out twenty thousand to impress me? Really?"

"Let's talk outside."

"No, we shouldn't talk outside. Everyone should know what a show-off you are."

"*Outside*, or leave me alone." There was something threatening in his voice, as if he would explode any second. He had been nice to her since their second encounter at the restaurant, but now he was more like what she had imagined him to be. A rich prick.

Without a word, she walked to the door. Matt followed her. They left the building and stopped around the corner where they wouldn't be seen by the people from the gym.

"Now, what the hell were you thinking to attack me in front of other people like that?" Matt asked.

"You better tell me why the hell you did it. To impress me?"

"What are you talking about?"

"About the donation to the shelter." She looked deep into his blue eyes. They widened. It had been him.

"I don't know what you're talking about."

"You don't? Let me help you remember the facts. Yesterday we spoke about the shelter. I told you I love this place. I also mentioned it had a tight budget." She paused for a second to gauge his reaction. It had been him. He wasn't a good liar. "I go to the shelter today to help James and Melinda and what do they tell me? An anonymous donor has given them twenty thousand dollars."

Matt pursed his lips. His nostrils flared and his eyes burned with anger.

"You really thought this would impress me? It's the most pitiful thing a guy has ever done to try to pick me up," she said.

"You're so full of yourself. Impress *you*? Leave me the hell alone," Matt said.

He turned on his feet and stormed off. She heard him open the door to the gym and enter the building.

That was odd. She expected him to explain himself, deny it or tell her he did it for the animals, not to impress her. But this?

Ashley plodded to her home feeling guilty, as if she had been the one in the wrong.

Chapter 7

Ashley opened the door to the shelter's office.

"Hi, Ashley," Melinda said. She wore glasses, which meant she had been working with paperwork. The shelter was a nonprofit organization, and there had always been a lot of paperwork to do.

"Hey, Melinda. What's the plan for today?"

"There's a lot to do."

"There's a lot to do," Ashley said with her. Melinda sent her a smile.

"We've been thinking with James how we should spend the money. We want to start with building a couple more kennels."

"So you want me to build them with you?"

"Sure, but not today. We need to go to the store and buy the building materials. Wood, screws, insulation and all that stuff only James know about."

"Where's James?"

"He's making a list. He's in Duke's kennel, taking measurements. We'd like to go to the store in a while. In the meantime, could you clean the pantry?"

"All right."

"Thank you, dear. I don't know what we would do without you."

Ashley smiled. It felt good to be appreciated by someone besides her sister.

When Melinda and James drove away, Ashley began cleaning the pantry. It was a small room in the back of the office with shelves and shelves of animal food. Dog food, cat food, rabbit food, it was all there. The shelves had been getting dusty from time to time, so one of the regular tasks was to remove all the food from the shelves and dust them off.

Usually it had been one of the tasks Ashley liked the least. However, after her conversation with Matt the day before, it felt good to work hard and forget about his angry reaction.

She removed the food, cleaned the shelves, put the food on the shelves again and swept the floor. When she was done, she was dripping with sweat. The heaviest bags of dog food weighed forty pounds. Ashley had been taking regular walks with Violet ever since she got her five years ago, but her physical endurance didn't translate to her physical strength. Each time she had to clean the pantry, she had sore arms for the next few days.

She lumbered to the office and collapsed on the sofa. Melinda and James should be back at any minute. Then she could go home and take a nap. Ashley laid her head on the old pillow with floral decorations. She felt something rustle under the pillow. She raised her head and picked up the pillow. A manila envelope lay squeezed in the corner of the sofa. It was probably some trash Melinda had forgotten to throw away. Out of curiosity, Ashley looked at the sender's address. "Red Maple Group, LLC," it said. She remembered the name of the company on Matt's business card. Blue Oak Technologies. Blue Oak Technologies, Red Maple Group. It had to be him, it was no coincidence the names were so similar.

She glanced at the postmark in the top right corner and opened her mouth. It was sent on Tuesday, three days before she met Matt on Friday. It had to be a donation from one of his companies, but he couldn't have done it to impress her.

A wave of embarrassment washed over her body. Why had she assumed he had done it to impress her? She should have checked it first before drawing any conclusions. Another poor judgment on her part.

As much as she hated the mere thought of doing it, she would have to apologize to Matt.

***

When Ashley got back home, she took a nap. Violet nudged her an hour later and woke her up. She rose from bed and took her dog for a walk. When she was back home, she realized it was time to go to the gym and check if Matt was there. She decided there was no sense in waiting. The sooner she did it, the sooner she would clear her mind.

Ashley went to the gym. She could see through the glass façade that Matt running alone on a treadmill. She entered the building and walked over to him.

"Hey. Do you have a minute?"

"I'm working out right now." He didn't even look in her direction.

"I'll wait outside."

There was no other way to leave the gym except for the back door. She doubted he would be so inclined to avoid her to ask the staff to let him out using the staff-only entrance.

Ashley sat at the bench across the gym and waited for Matt. She pondered how to apologize to him. Had it really been her fault that she had always had an overly sensitive detector of womanizers? It wouldn't have been the first time a guy spent money to impress her. Spencer had been a rare exception. Maybe that's why she found him attractive. Ashley took her mind off Spencer and looked at the gym.

She saw Matt getting off the treadmill. He glanced in her direction and shook his head. Then he disappeared into the lockers room.

When ten minutes passed and he still hadn't left the building, Ashley thought he really chose to ask the staff the embarrassing question instead of talking with her. But then he emerged from the locker room and headed to the front door. Ashley felt her hands trembling.

"What do you want to talk about?" he said. His forceful gaze made her shy.

"I want to apologize."

Matt raised his eyebrows.

"I want to apologize for yesterday. I saw the check had been sent on Tuesday, three days before you learned I worked there. Why didn't you tell me?"

"There was no point. I've learned a long time ago there's no point arguing with the self-righteous."

He sounded nothing like the Matt she had been speaking to in the woods. His cold words made her freeze.

"I'm so sorry. I'm too sensitive when it comes to these things," she said.

"I sent it anonymously so that nobody would know about it. You come to the gym and announce it to everybody. I had to come up with a story to make them believe I had nothing to do with it."

"I'm—"

"I don't want to be judged by people by the money I have. That's why I moved here. It gets tiring after a while to constantly be on the lookout for freeloaders."

"I won't tell anybody. You have my word."

"That's a relief." His face muscles relaxed.

"I'm so sorry for my outburst."

"Apology accepted."

"Thank you so much for the donation. It will change everything for the shelter. We're going to build new kennels, repair the old ones and fix other stuff. It will make a huge difference."

"I'm glad to hear that."

"I'd like to make up for my stupid behavior yesterday. I'm a quite good cook. I could cook something for you?"

"Cook for me?"

"You come to the restaurant every single day, anyway. I can cook much better carbonara than they do. Different cuisines, too."

"French?"

"I know a couple recipes."

"*Pot-au-feu*?"

"My sister loves when I cook it."

"So, when should I come?"

All her tense muscles relaxed when she saw a wide smile on his face.

Chapter 8

"I'm running a bit late. I didn't notice I didn't have leeks. I had to rush to the store to get it," Ashley said.

Matt was at her home at seven on the dot. She was mad at herself for being in the middle of the cooking when he knocked on her door.

"No worries. Let me help you."

"You're my guest. I said I would cook it for you."

"It's okay. I'm hopeless with cooking, but I can at least chop some vegetables."

"Okay. Could you please cut the carrots and turnips?"

"Sure."

He rolled the sleeves of his blue shirt. She glanced at his forearms. He had been working out for much longer than a couple of weeks with Richard.

"Where's the cutting board?" he asked.

"I'm sorry. Right over there." She pointed to a countertop in the corner of the kitchen, right beside the window.

Matt grabbed the cutting board, put it on the table and started chopping vegetables. Violet lay in her usual place on a thick blanket under the table. Ashley was surprised when Violet welcomed Matt in the door. When someone visited Ashley, Violet usually hid somewhere in the house and emerged only after making sure it was someone she had already known.

Ashley cooked the soup and hummed to herself. Julia rarely visited Ashley at home. She was too busy with the gas station and her own family. After Spencer moved out, or rather after he was kicked out by Ashley, few people visited her house. It felt nice to have a guest.

"How did you learn how to cook?" Matt asked. He stood at the table and chopped carrots.

"I just tried a lot of recipes. Some worked, some didn't."

"I've never been good at cooking. Frankly speaking, I'm hopeless. That's why I eat out."

"Azure isn't the best restaurant in town, you know."

"Maybe it isn't, but it sure has the best waitresses." Ashley felt happy to hear Matt was no longer angry at her. His cold demeanor the day before frightened her.

"Hopefully not for long."

"You want to quit?"

"I wanted to quit before I had even started working there."

Matt chuckled.

"So, what do you want to do when you quit?"

"Get more freelance gigs, work at home."

"I can help you with that. I've worked with a lot of Web designers. I know people who might need your services."

"Thank you. I appreciate the offer."

"But seriously, let me call some people. I'll see what I can do. It would be a win-win for both of you, as long as you're good."

"I can send you my portfolio."

"Sure. That would be great."

Ashley sensed he really wanted to help and didn't expect anything in return. Usually, she would suspect it was just another way to get in her pants, but she told herself she had to put an end to judging people.

But then again, with men, you never knew. Spencer had been such a faithful boyfriend, after all. And then she saw him banging her colleague in his old Acura right beside the forest. And then she learned it hadn't been his first time cheating on her.

"Where should I put it?" Matt asked. He walked over to her with a cutting board and chopped vegetables.

"Right here." She pointed to a countertop on her right. He walked behind her. A light scent of oranges lingered in the air. A fitting fragrance for a man like Matt.

"Ten to fifteen minutes and it will be ready," she said.

"No worries, I'm not in a hurry."

Fifteen minutes later, they sat at the dark brown kitchen table Ashley inherited from her parents when they died three years ago. It had always been one of her favorite places in her small, but cozy house.

"Do you have anything for Violet?" Matt asked. Violet sat beside him and put her paw on his lap. The begging look in her eyes was unmistakable.

"She's always such a beggar." Ashley opened one of the drawers and gave Violet a biscuit shaped like a bone. The dog trotted away with the biscuit in her mouth.

"Oh my God, this is delicious," Matt exclaimed.

"I'm happy you like it."

"Like it? I love it. I haven't eaten better *pot-au-feu* in my life."

"Thank you." Ashley blushed. She wasn't used to compliments about her cooking skills. Most guys complimented her hazel eyes, long legs, or thick hair. Except for James and Spencer when she had been with him, no man said anything nice about something else than her looks.

"How's Duke?" she asked to change the topic.

"I'm happy to report he's been getting less and less timid. He's no longer so afraid of other dogs. It will probably take much more time to teach him to stop being so afraid of people, though."

Ashley smiled. The way Matt spoke about Duke indicated he really cared about the dog. She had been working at the shelter for long enough to understand there were people who simply liked dogs and there were people who loved them. Matt was certainly in the latter group.

"I'm glad to hear that. You gave him a chance he would have never gotten otherwise."

"There must be other people who adopt older dogs."

"Unfortunately, no. I'd say that ninety percent of people come to the shelter looking for puppies."

"It's sad."

"It is. At least the dogs don't have it that bad. And now, some of them will get new kennels."

Matt smiled and focused on his bowl of soup. Ashley sensed he hadn't been used to hearing words of gratitude. She wondered if she could be as humble as he was and donate money anonymously.

"Tell me something about the woods. Are there any places I should check out? You seem to be pretty knowledgeable about the woods around the town," he said.

"There are a few places you should check out. There's a small creek flowing through the forest. It's about fifteen minutes away from here. There's a place where you can sit down on a bench right beside it."

"Sounds interesting."

"There's also a beautiful glade in the middle of the forest, but it's far away from the town. At least two hours of walking."

"Another place to add to my list."

"There's also a hill from which you can see the entire town. It's also quite far away, but the view is spectacular. I like to go there at least once a week, but it's not a dog-friendly path. Violet gets exhausted."

"I would love to go there."

There was so much excitement in his voice, as if she had been describing to him the Seven Wonders of the Ancient World.

"Would you take me there? Would you show me all the places? I guess you don't have GPS coordinates for all of them."

She chuckled.

"You're a survivalist, right? Shouldn't you know how to find these places with no help?"

"A little company would be nice. I can't take Duke on such a long walk, especially since you say that even Violet gets exhausted."

"Sure, why not." To her surprise, she didn't mind showing him around at all. His enthusiasm was contagious. It had been a long time since she had spent time with someone other than James, Melinda and Julia.

"Perfect. Just let me know when you're free and I'll be ready."

"I'm free on Wednesday. I have a day off at work."

"Works for me."

The rest of the dinner made Ashley realize Matt was a funny, friendly and interesting person. She liked how attentive he was when she spoke. Most guys she had met in her life were more interested in her breasts than what she had to say. It was a welcome change to speak with someone who cared about what she said. Ashley realized she had begun to like him.

"Thank you for the dinner," he said. Ashley accompanied him to the door. "The restaurant is no match for your cooking."

"I'm glad to hear that."

"See you on Wednesday."

Ashley began to approach him to hug him and stopped in her tracks. He had still been a stranger. What was she thinking? She extended her hand instead. They shook hands. Matt opened the door and left.

Ashley went to the kitchen. Matt walked down the street. The street lamp illuminated his face. He was smiling.

Ashley was about to turn around when she heard the noise of a car engine. An old Acura sped down the neighborhood street.

Had it been Spencer's car?

Chapter 9

The path to Maple Hill had always been a long trip for Ashley. It had always taken her at least one hour to get there. With Matt, she could've sworn the entire journey had lasted less than fifteen minutes.

Ashley realized there had been much more to Matt than just being an ex-CEO of a large company. In fact, he had been avoiding talking about business and preferred getting to know her.

She realized how much she had missed a nice conversation. Julia had always been busy. She could always talk with her, but fifteen minutes had been usually the most she could give her. James and Melinda had always been friendly, but besides the shelter, they didn't have any other topics for conversation.

"Are we there yet?" Matt asked. He pointed to a hill about half a mile in front of them.

Her eyes wandered over his fit body. He was dressed in olive pants and a navy polo shirt. Even though Ashley had always thought that a man looked best in a well-tailored suit, she liked his simple, casual outfits. But then again, everything looked good on a handsome person.

"It's the second hill after this one. Five minutes and we'll be there."

She gazed at his face. He looked like a kid in a candy store. After she broke up with Spencer, Ashley had forgotten how to be happy with the little things. Matt, unknowingly to him, had started teaching her how to change her attitude.

Five minutes later, they climbed the hill. Old thick maples covered almost the entire hill with the exception of a small opening where you could stand and admire the town below. Ashley had been always wondering if someone had planted the trees this way or if it had been just a coincidence.

The entire hill was covered in grass. She liked the gentle feel of grass underneath her feet. She took off her shoes and put them near a large flat stone.

"Wow. Wow. Wow," Matt exclaimed.

She chuckled. He sounded like a kid trapped in the body of an adult.

"Isn't it the most beautiful view in the world?" he said. "I mean, look around." He took in the view.

She walked over to him and looked below. The small town covered an area of a few square miles. The view of the town was partly blocked by the forest and trees that grew on the other side of the hill. It was still possible to see almost all of Maple Hills, except for one of the newest neighborhoods.

Ashley could make out her small white house with a light gray roof. Julia's gas station was also visible from the hill. Ashley saw a tiny red speck walking into the station's building. It was too far away to be sure, but it could have been Julia. She had always liked wearing red dresses.

Ashley left Matt standing on the top of the hill. She walked to a large flat stone and sat down on it. Whenever it was sunny, she had always lain on top of it to get a tan. A warm feeling crept into her belly when she remembered she had sometimes taken off her top and lain on the stone half-naked. She chuckled when she imagined how Matt would have reacted if he saw her lying on the stone with bare breasts.

She scolded herself for her crazy dirty thoughts. What the hell had she been thinking? How had she even started thinking about it?

"Hey, Ashley, is it your restaurant right over there?" Matt asked.

She rose up and walked over to him.

"Where?"

"Over there." He pointed to a small red brick building a few blocks away from the gas station.

Ashley had never seen the restaurant from the hill. Not that she even looked for it. She strained her eyes and took a step forward.

Something slipped under her foot. A strong hand squeezed Ashley's arm like a vise and helped her regain balance. A small stone rolled down the hill. If it wasn't for Matt, she would have rolled along with the stone.

She exhaled a long breath and took a few steps back. Matt still held her trembling arm.

"That was a close one," he said.

She gazed into his blue eyes, bluer than everything she had ever seen in her life. "Thank you, Matt."

"No worries. I wouldn't like to see you down there with twisted limbs." He pointed to the base of the hill where a small stone had just joined a large group of stones that were gathered there.

Matt realized he had been still holding her arm and loosened his grip. His fingers brushed her biceps. Ashley felt a shiver down her spine.

They stood on top of the hill and looked at each other. She noticed a change in his deep blue eyes. Had it been a yearning desire or was she just imagining things?

Ashley glanced at his lips and gazed back into his eyes. He leaned forward and brushed his nose over her forehead. She smelled a familiar scent of oranges. His lips pressed against hers. She closed his eyes. A burning desire spread over her entire body. She opened her mouth and let his warm tongue in. She moaned with pleasure. It had been so long since she had been kissing with someone like that.

Matt pulled out his tongue.

"Don't stop," she whispered. She placed her palms on his smooth cheeks and pulled him back in.

He put his strong arms around her. His tongue swirled around hers. She lightly bit his lip. His groan broke the perfect silence and made Ashley kiss him with even more passion. She slid her right hand down his shirt and ran a hand over his belly. Ashley slid her fingers across his metal belt buckle. She wanted him right there, right now.

Ashley heard someone shouting from below. "We're almost there," a voice said.

Matt broke the embrace and smiled at her.

"Did you say it was a secret place?"

She took a long breath and sighed. "I didn't. People rarely come here, especially on a weekday."

"They couldn't have chosen a better moment." He had dilated pupils and his cheeks gained a red hue. Oh God, how much she wanted to kiss him again and again and again.

"Let's get going," he said. "Can you walk?"

"Very funny. It's a shame you can't see yourself and your rosy cheeks," she said.

He took her hand in his. Ashley walked over to the stone and put on her shoes. On her way down the hill, they passed a group of teenagers.

They walked down the hill in silence. Ashley had already forgotten how pleasant it was to hold someone's hand and enjoy a walk together. Matt hadn't commented on what they had been doing on top of the hill, so she didn't comment on it, either.

"The next time we go to the woods, you have to show me the two other places. The creek and the glade," he said.

"All right. I have a lot of work this week, but I should be free early next week."

"Perfect. Works for me."

They walked together across the woods. The birds chirped around them. Afternoon sunlight shone through the leaves. It seemed as if the whole world radiated with energy.

Ashley had last seen the world in such bright colors five years ago, when she had first met Spencer. This time, though, the colors felt much more intense. Ashley felt as if she had been a teenager. Matt's presence filled her with joy she hadn't even considered she had in herself. And to think she had hated him just a couple weeks ago.

They almost reached the edge of the woods when Matt came to a halt.

"What?" she asked.

He pressed her against a tree and kissed her with raw passion. Her legs became wobbly.

"Would you like to come over for some tea?" she asked when he pulled his face away.

"Sure. I would love to."

Matt had as much talent in bed as he had with kissing.

Chapter 10

Three weeks had passed since their first kiss. Ashley's life went from shades of gray to full color in high definition. Matt had helped her realize how dull her life was before she had met him. Spencer had made her distrustful not only of men, but also of people in general. Now she had her life back.

Each day, she and Matt took their dogs on a walk together. Matt taught her some useful survival skills. To her surprise, she enjoyed learning the skills she had always thought were reserved for crazies.

As Matt had promised, he also introduced her to some of his friends who were interested in her services. Thanks to his referrals, Ashley had enough ongoing work to quit her job at the restaurant. Which, to Courtney's shock, she did.

"How do I look?" Ashley asked Violet. She stood in front of a mirror and tried on yet another dress. Matt invited her to his house in the evening. She had to look perfect.

Violet titled her head to the side.

"You don't like it?"

The dog laid her head on the floor and closed her eyes.

"I guess that means no."

She tried on a few more dresses. She liked a red summer dress the most. Julia had always looked stunning in her red dress, so it had to look great on Ashley, too.

Ashley glanced at the watch and noticed it was already six. She was supposed to be at Matt's at six thirty.

She stormed out of the room and opened a shoe cabinet standing in the hallway near the front door. Light brown heels would fit perfectly. She went to her bedroom and opened the wardrobe. She left the room with a brown handbag on her arm.

When she arrived at Matt's place, she was surprised to see an old Jeep in his driveway. Did he have a guest?

"Hey, babe. Come in," Matt said. He put his hands around her waist and kissed her. "You look absolutely stunning."

"Thank you. You don't look so bad yourself." He wore a well-fitted blue dress shirt and a pair of gray slacks.

Duke emerged from the room at the end of the corridor. Ashley crouched to pet him. The dog had changed so much she could barely recognize him. He had always been a timid dog who didn't enjoy the presence of other people. Matt had somehow taught him how to trust people again. Just like he had taught Ashley.

"Everything is ready. Let's go to the dining room." He motioned her to follow him. It was the first time she had been to his house. Ashley was surprised how simple and minimalistic it was. She expected a rich interior with a lot of expensive furniture and art, but his house was anything but that.

She liked Matt for his humbleness. As he said to her once, money meant freedom to him, and too many possessions limited his independence.

Matt led her to a spacious dining room. It was painted white, which made the room appear even bigger. In the middle of the room was a dark brown wooden dining table. There were six chairs around it. Glass sliding door separated the room from the garden outside. Two white lamps hung from the ceiling above the table.

Ashley smelled something delicious in the air. She was curious to see what was underneath the stainless steel food covers on the table.

"What is that?"

"Please sit down first. I'll be your waiter today."

Ashley sat down at the table. Matt approached her from behind and covered her eyes with one hand. She heard the clanking of the metal cover.

“Ready?” he asked.

“Ready.”

He removed his hand from her face. On a plate was a piece of one of the most delicious-looking lasagnas she has ever seen in her life. Three layers of lasagna were topped off with some kind of tomato sauce and sprinkled with fresh parsley.

Matt walked around the table and sat across her.

“You told me you couldn’t cook,” she said.

“I couldn’t. But I learned some recipes. And who could better judge my efforts than you?”

“It looks delicious.”

“I’m more curious about how it tastes.”

She put a small piece in her mouth. Matt looked at her with anticipation in his eyes.

“And?”

“Was it really one of the first things you’ve ever cooked?”

“I’m not sure how to answer this question. I’ve been cooking it every other day for the last two weeks.”

She chuckled. “You really did?”

“How else could I learn how to make a perfect lasagna? Anyway, what do you think?”

“I think it’s perfect. Way better than what they serve at Azure.”

He exhaled a breath of relief. “I’m so glad to hear that. I was afraid you wouldn’t like it.”

"I hope you cooked a lot of it. I'm not leaving the table until I eat all the lasagna you have in the house, as long as it's been cooked by you."

"My lasagna is yours."

Ashley savored the food. Matt was a man of many talents. He was a great teacher of survival skills, he could dance, speak Spanish, and cook incredible lasagna. And his bedroom skills… She shifted her mind to a different thought before her cheeks flushed with blood.

"Whose car is that Jeep?" she asked.

"It's mine."

"What happened to the Cadillac?"

"I sold it."

"Why? I thought you liked it."

"Not so much. I had to drive it back in L.A. to give off that vibe of success. Here, I'm free to drive what I want. I prefer something more low-key."

"I've never thought of you as a Jeep person."

"I've always wanted to have an old Jeep and tinker around with it. I'm retired, after all. I figured it was high time to make this dream come true."

"You need to take me for a ride, then."

"Sure. After dinner."

Ashley grabbed her fork and started eating the food like a starved dog. Matt burst out laughing. Oh, how much she enjoyed his carefree laugh. And how much happiness this laugh of his had introduced in her life.

When they finished lasagna, Matt told her to wait. He had another surprise for her.

"Close your eyes," he said from the corridor.

Ashley closed her eyes. She heard him enter the room. He put something on the table in front of her.

"You can open them now."

She opened her eyes. A perfect piece of tiramisu was on her plate, with much more of the cake on a long dessert plate in the middle of the table.

"I figured we could have a little Italian-themed dinner. Do you like it?" Matt said.

"Don't say you made it by yourself," she said.

"I did."

"Matt, this looks perfect. Now let me taste it."

She grabbed a dessert fork and put a small piece of the cake in her mouth. She felt full after the lasagna. When she tasted the first bite of the dessert, she forgot about her full stomach.

"I know I'm repeating myself, but Matt, this is the best tiramisu I've ever eaten."

"I'm happy to hear that. Frankly speaking, it was much easier to learn than the lasagna."

"But it's equally good. If not better. No offense to your lasagna."

He chuckled. "No offense taken."

His cell phone interrupted their conversation. He excused himself and left the room.

Matt came back to the room a few minutes later. He had pursed lips. Ashley saw a flash of anger in his eyes.

"Is everything okay? You look rattled."

"No, it's fine. Just a call from my ex-partner."

"Anything important? Do you want to talk about it?"

"Actually, would you mind if we changed the plan and cut our dinner short? I can take you for a ride on another day."

"Okay." There was something weird in his behavior, as if he was afraid of something.

"Is it really okay?"

"Sure, don't worry. It's fine."

She rose up from the chair.

"Would you like to take some of the tiramisu with you?" he asked.

"Of course. How could I not?"

He went to the kitchen and reappeared after a minute with a plastic food container.

"You don't want any?" Ashley asked when she noticed he put the entire cake in the container.

"Don't worry about me. I've eaten lasagna and tiramisu every other day for the last two weeks."

Matt joked, but Ashley knew he had been upset.

"Matt, are you sure you don't want to talk about something?"

"Like what?"

"The call?" She hoped she wouldn't anger him with her duh-like tone. Something had thrown him off balance and he struggled to keep it from showing on his face.

"No, everything is really fine. Nothing to talk about. Just some business issues."

He closed the lid of the container and accompanied her to the front door.

"Matt, if there's anything you'd like to talk about with me, I'm always there for you."

"I know. Thank you, Ashley."

She left his house and walked home pondering what could have rattled him so much.

Chapter 11

The next day after the Italian dinner at Matt's place, Ashley heard the doorbell rang. She hoped it was Matt and that he would finally explain what happened on the day before. She opened the door without first checking who was outside. It was a mistake.

"Hi, Ashley," Spencer said.

He looked like he had spent a better part of an hour in the bathroom preparing to look his best. He was dressed in gray slacks and a white dress shirt. His short brown hair was combed. He also had light brown stubble on his cheeks. Ashley smelled a light scent of cologne in the air.

"What the hell did I tell you the last time? Leave me alone."

"Ashley, we need to talk."

"There's nothing to talk about. I think we've already established that."

"I think there is something to talk about. Your boyfriend."

"Don't you even talk about Matt."

"Why not?"

"Get. The. Hell. Out."

"Okay."

He descended the porch steps. When Ashley was about to shut the door, he turned around on his heels.

"Hey, by the way, have you heard that somebody wants to sue the shelter?"

"Do what?"

"Someone has donated a lot of money to the shelter. Now it seems it was just a ploy to have leverage against Brookes'."

"What the hell are you talking about?"

"Ask your boyfriend. He should know. Have a nice day." Spencer waved to her and got into his car. Why the hell was he so happy?

Ashley went back to her home and called Melinda.

"Melinda, I've heard some rumors about the shelter."

"It's true."

"What is true?" Melinda's grave voice sent a shiver down Ashley's back.

"We're blackmailed."

"You're what? I'll be there right away."

***

"Tell me what happened," Ashley said. She sat in the office with James and Melinda. The couple sat together at the sofa with their heads hung low. They reminded Ashley of some of the older dogs that had been living in the shelter for a few months already.

"We received a call from a lawyer," Melinda said.

"Somebody from Delaware," James added.

"He asked us how much money we would like to get for the shelter and the school. I said we don't want to sell it," Melinda said. Her hands trembled.

"And then he said that one of his associates has sent us twenty thousand dollars as an upfront payment."

"An upfront payment? It was a donation," Ashley said. She wanted to speak with Matt right away, but first she had to get the facts from the horse's mouth.

"Turns out there's a legal loophole or something like that. He spoke in legalese. I couldn't really grasp what he had said," Melinda said.

"How much have we spent so far? We can return the money, right?" Ashley said.

"We've spent over ten thousand. Besides, he said we can't do that," James said.

"And why's that so?"

"He said that if we don't accept their generous offer, they will sue us," Melinda said.

"Sue us for what? On what basis?"

"He threw around some legal terms. He said they had a team of lawyers ready to, let me quote it for you, 'litigate the shit out of us.'"

Ashley felt her blood boiling.

"He said that even if we won against them, it would take months to get it settled. Don't even get me started on the legal costs. They can afford it. We can't."

"What's their offer?" Ashley asked.

"Ashley, we don't want to sell our life's work," James replied.

"I know. Just tell me what he said." Ashley had to know everything before she would go to Matt.

"Two hundred thousand," he said.

"Two hundred thousand? Are they out of their minds?"

"He said it's their final offer."

"Why do they even want this place, anyway?"

"He mentioned their 'research team' had learned it's a perfect place for a country golf course."

"A golf course? There's not enough place here for this."

"That's why they also want to buy the part of the woods that belongs to us and clear it."

"Everything for two hundred thousand? I can't believe it."

"We have two weeks to make a decision," Melinda said.

"What happens after two weeks?"

"They sue us and do everything they can to close the shelter and the school."

***

Ashley didn't bother calling Matt. She walked straight to his house and knocked on his door.

"Matt. We need to talk."

"I'm coming. What's going on?"

She heard the door unlock. Matt stared at her with confusion on his face.

"Do you have something to tell me?"

"I'm sorry. I don't know what you are talking about."

"The shelter. The donation. The call from the lawyer."

He acted as if he hadn't known anything about it.

"Ashley, let's sit down and you'll explain everything to me, okay?"

"I… Okay."

"Come in and tell me what is going on."

He let her in and motioned her to go to the living room at the right. Matt walked to the coffee table and closed the laptop that lay on top of it. He sat down at the sofa and motioned her to sit with him. Ashley chose the armchair.

"Do you want anything to drink?"

"No. Just explain everything to me."

"Ashley, I have no idea what you're talking about. Please tell me what is going on."

Ashley told him what she had heard from James and Melinda. When she finished, Matt clenched his fists and pursed his lips. His face was reddened with anger.

"Now, what can you tell me about it?"

"Do you remember the call yesterday? It was my ex-partner. I spoke with him about our company."

"What does it have to do with this situation?"

Matt glared at her. "Let me speak."

"I'm sorry." He looked so frightening when he was mad.

"The LLC that sent the money to the shelter belongs to me and him. I had full rights to send my share of income to the shelter, but he argued with me. 'Getting too sensitive on your retirement?' he said. That pissed me off."

Ashley felt relief. "So, was it his way of getting back at you?"

"Never in a million years would I have thought he would do something like this. I vouch my partners. I can't believe he did it."

"You can call him and ask him, can't you?"

Matt pulled out his cell phone from the pocket and made a call. Ashley stared at his left hand clenched in a fist. Matt had been vibrating with anger.

"Nobody is picking up the phone."

"Call again."

He dialed the number again. Matt tapped his fingers on the coffee table.

"I will keep trying. If he has done it, I will make his life miserable."

The coldness in his voice sent a cold shiver down her spine. It had also made her realize Matt couldn't have been behind this situation.

"Keep calling. I need to find Spencer."

"Who's Spencer?"

"My ex-boyfriend. He knocked on my door today and told me about the shelter. I want to find out how he had learned about it."

"Let me know if you learn anything useful. I will keep calling Jamie in the meantime."

Ashley rose from the armchair. Matt followed her. When they reached the front door, she turned on her heels and gave him a kiss.

"I will call you as soon as I speak with Jamie."

"Thank you. I will ask Spencer and my sister if they know something about it."

"Say hello to Julia from me."

"Will do."

She opened the door and stopped in her tracks.

"Matt?"

"Yes?"

"We will overcome it. Together."

"I know."

Chapter 12

"Spencer? Pick up the phone. We need to talk," Ashley said to the phone. Her only reply was the beep of the voicemail. It had been her fifth try to reach him. What was going on? It was six o'clock, so even if he had found a new job, he would already be at home.

She paced her room. Violet sat in the corner and watched her nervous movements.

"Hey, Violet, do you want to go out?"

The dog rose up and trotted over to her with a wagging tail.

"I guess that means yes."

A walk with Violet would do her good. She would clear her mind and consider different possibilities.

She leashed Violet and opened the door. Spencer stood on her porch, still in his sharp attire. He gave her a wide smile, as if he was proud to stand on her porch and not be kicked out the instant she had seen him. Violet barked at him. When Spencer had been living with them, Violet liked him. After he had left, she was even more aggressive toward him than Ashley.

"I've been calling you for two hours," she said.

"I was busy."

"Busy? I called you a few minutes ago and you didn't pick up."

"Because I was on my way here. You said it was something important."

"How did you learn about the shelter?"

"So now you know."

"Now I want to know how you had known about it before I did."

"Did you talk with your boyfriend? I heard there was a big fight between you two." The tone of his voice reminded Ashley of a snake.

There was something off about it. She decided to play along and act as if she was mad at Matt.

"It's none of your concern."

"Oh, look who's getting angry at her beloved boyfriend now. I told you he wasn't as goody-goody as you had thought."

"Answer my question. How did you heard about the shelter?"

"Rumors."

"Rumors?"

"Ashley, it's a small town. It's not my problem you don't leave your home often enough to have friends."

"So who told you about it?"

"What does it matter? What matters is that now you finally know who Matt really is."

"How did you know that Matt had made a donation to the shelter?"

"Too many questions. Like I said before, it doesn't matter. Have a nice day." He turned around and sauntered to his car. He was too happy about the situation. Ashley had to find out what role he had played in it.

She pulled out her cell phone from the pocket and called Julia.

"Julia, can I come over?"

"Sure. I'm free in an hour."

"I'll be there."

She hung up and closed the door to her house. She had enough time for a quick walk with Violet.

When she returned from her walk, she changed into more presentable clothes than an old pair of jeans and a white top. Julia had always liked to keep it classy. She scolded her for wearing, as her sister called them, 'too comfortable' clothes.

Ashley changed into a light blue summer dress. Julia bought it for her. It had always brightened Julia's day to see Ashley in a dress she had bought for her sister. Ashley needed all the help she could get to convince Julia of her plan.

***

"What a nice dress, Ashley. Would you like anything to drink?" Julia said. She was in a good mood. Ashley hoped it had been good enough to convince Julia to help her.

"A glass of water, please."

"Sure."

Julia's office was dominated by a large desk with layers and layers of paper on top of it. In the corner of the room was a small kitchenette. Julia walked to the countertop and poured Ashley water from a pitcher.

"Would you like some ice?"

"Yes, please."

Ashley walked over to a small fridge and opened the freezer. She grabbed a couple of ice cubes from the freezer and dropped them into Ashley's cup.

"Thank you," Ashley said.

"Now, what's up? I know this look. You'd like me to do something for you, right?"

"Guilty as charged."

"No need to keep up appearances. How can I help you?"

"I have a… situation with Spencer."

"Don't tell me you broke up with Matt and hooked up with this idiot again."

"No, it's not about that." She stopped to collect her thoughts.

"Then what's wrong? What's the situation?"

"Do you still have this GPS tracker you used to find out if George had really gone to the conference a year or so ago?"

Julia blushed. Only her sister had known she spied on her husband.

"I… I do have it somewhere around here."

"What about the voice recorder?"

"It's in the same place with the tracker."

"Could you… lend them to me?"

"Ashley, what are you up to?"

"I have some… suspicions about Spencer."

"About what exactly?"

Ashley weighed her words. She wasn't sure if she wanted to involve her sister in this.

"Ashley, you can trust me. You know that."

"Have you heard about the situation with the shelter?"

"About what? The donation? Richard told me you had built some nice new kennels."

"Well, there is a problem with it."

Ashley told Julia all she had learned since the morning from Spencer, James, Melinda, and Matt.

"And you think Spencer was behind it?"

"Matt told me that this partner of his couldn't have done it."

"But he's been calling him, anyway."

"Only because I insisted. After I spoke with Spencer, I think it was just a coincidence about Matt's partner."

Ashley's cell phone rang. It was Matt.

"Hey, babe. I spoke with Jamie. He's on a vacation in Mexico. He had no idea about it."

"He could lie to you."

"I triple checked it. I called his secretary, my other partner and his accountant. They all confirmed he's on a vacation and there are no plans related to Maple Hills."

"So it couldn't have been him."

"We talked about the donation. He said he had just taunted me. I believe him. What about Spencer?"

"I spoke with him. I think he could be behind all of this, but I can't exactly wrap my head around it."

"Do you want me to come over? We can talk about it together."

"Give me some time. I need to investigate it by myself."

Ashley hung up.

"See, I told you," she said to Julia.

"So, what's your plan?"

"I want to find out what Spencer has been up to recently."

"And a GPS tracker would help you accomplish it how exactly?"

"Somebody called the shelter. It couldn't have been Spencer, as Melinda would have known his voice."

"You think he has a partner."

"Exactly. I'm no James Bond. I couldn't follow him in a car, even if I had one."

"I think I have something that could help you. Come on."

Julia rose up from her chair and motioned Ashley to follow her. They walked down the corridor and entered a small dimly lit room with a single desk and walls decorated with outdated calendars and a poster of a half-naked blonde model. A light scent of cigarettes mixed with Old Spice lingered in the air.

A fifty-something man dressed in a blue uniform of a security guard sat at the desk. He watched the video from six cameras showing the gas station and the store. He turned in his black office chair and widened his eyes.

"Mrs. Pine, Ms. Madison, I'm sorry. I didn't expect you here."

"It's okay, Fred. Could you give us a minute here alone?"

"Of course."

He rose up from the chair and left them in the security room alone.

Ashley pointed to the poster of a blonde supermodel.

"Is that okay with you?"

Julia shrugged.

"Let's get to business," Julia said. She sat at the desk and opened a program on the computer. She clicked on the rewind icon. The timestamp went from seven o'clock to eight in the morning.

"There we go."

She clicked the play button. Ashley saw a black Lexus pulling into the station. A fifty-something man with light gray hair and a gray suit of the same shade left the car and walked to the pump. He paid for the gas and refueled his car. Ashley saw a man sitting on the passenger's seat.

"Is it Spencer sitting shotgun?" Julia asked.

"It is." He was dressed in the same outfit as he had worn when he knocked on her door in the morning. "Whose car is that?"

"A scumbag lawyer from Portland, Oregon. Peter Pattison. I had the doubtful pleasure of dealing with him in the past."

"How did you even see a random black Lexus pulling into the station?"

"I was explaining something to the clerk when they pulled in. I glanced outside, and I thought I saw Spencer in there. It was strange to see him in Pattison's car, so I remembered it."

"Do you think it was this Pattison guy helping Spencer?"

"I would be surprised if it wasn't him. Talk with Spencer. You now know what he's been up to."

"Could you lend me this voice recorder?"

"Ashley, do you know it's illegal to record other people without their permission?"

"And since when is it legal to blackmail them?"

"You have a point."

"So, does that mean yes?"

Julia shrugged, but nodded. They walked back to the office. Julia opened the bottom drawer of her desk and pulled out a small device.

"Do you know how to use it?" Julia asked.

"It's not exactly rocket science. Thanks, sis."

"Good luck."

Ashley walked to the door to the office. She opened it and turned over her shoulder.

"Julia?"

Julia lifted her eyes off the files spread out on the table. "What's up?"

"Matt says 'hi.'"

Julia smiled.

"He's a good guy, Ashley."

"He is." Ashley raised her hand in which she held the voice recorder. "Thanks again, sis."

"Take care. And don't get in trouble."

Ashley wasn't so sure she could avoid it.

Chapter 13

Ashley left the gas station and strode to Spencer's house. She would record their entire conversation and hope it was enough to blackmail him. She didn't look forward to it, but if there was no other way to save the shelter, she had to fight fire with fire.

Ashley had no doubt it had been Spencer's plan all along to make her fight with Matt and leave him. Spencer had been like a dog in the manger. What he overlooked was the fact that Ashley had relearned how to trust men.

She turned left into the Spencer's neighborhood when her phone rang. It was Matt.

"Ashley, it was Spencer," he said. His voice was grim.

"What?"

"A few minutes ago I received a call. The caller told me to meet with him at the bench in the forest. He said it's about you and the shelter."

"I'm going with you."

"No way," Matt said in a raised voice. "Ashley, it's a perfect scenario. He thinks you're angry at me. What did you tell him?"

"He said he had heard about our big fight. I played along."

"Ashley, you're a genius. Now he wants to put the final nail into the coffin. Only he doesn't know we're together against him."

"What's you plan?"

"I'm about to meet him at the bench at nine. It will be dark, so you can hide in the forest."

"And I can record him."

"Record?"

"I borrowed a voice recorder from my sister. It's top-notch quality. We can use it to blackmail him."

"Ashley..."

"Matt, it's the only way. Sometimes you have to fight fire with fire."

"I—"

"Trust me on this. I've known Spencer for many years, and I know how he has changed in the last months."

There was a long pause.

"Matt?"

"Make sure he can't see you."

"I know the place like the back of my hand. I'm going there now." She turned around. "Make him confess what he has done."

"What's his surname?"

"Cross. Make him say it, or at least confirm it."

"Roger that, Ms. Bond."

Ashley chuckled.

"Matt, be careful."

"You too. See you at nine. We'll get him."

***

Ashley hid behind the thick shrubs a few feet away from the bench. There was no way she could be seen from the bench or from the trail leading to it, as long as she didn't sneeze or do something equally stupid.

She sat on a makeshift pillow she had put together from a couple of thicker branches and moss. It was one of the survival tricks Matt had taught her. It turned out survival did have practical use.

Ashley was glad she had helped her sister buy the recorder. It was an extremely sensitive device that could record audio in crystal clear quality from twenty feet. Sitting in her hiding place, she could record the entire conversation without worrying over the quality. Worst comes to worst, it would hold in court.

In court. How could have Spencer changed so much was beyond Ashley. Or perhaps he had always been this way, and she had only learned it when she caught him cheating on her.

Ashley saw a tiny speck of light coming from the edge of the forest. It had to be a flashlight. The question was whether it was Spencer or Matt. She was afraid to pull out her cell phone. The light from the screen could give away her position. Matt had taught her that one of the dumbest things to do in the darkness when you were hiding from someone was to light a cigarette.

The light from the flashlight flashed around the bench, the stream beside it and across the trees in front of Ashley. Then she saw the light illuminating her hiding spot. She held her breath and tensed all her muscles.

And then the light was gone.

"I'm here. It's all clear. He should be here in fifteen minutes or so." It was Spencer's voice. "Sure, Pete, I'll pat him down. Relax."

So it had been the lawyer. Julia was right.

"Don't worry. He's so afraid he probably pissed in his pants when I called him. He will listen."

Matt had been right, too. Spencer wanted to blackmail him. It felt surreal to her and ridiculous at the same time. Spencer had cheated on her with at least three different women. When she had broken up with him and was free to spend the time with anybody she wanted, he became jealous. Did he really expect her to get back with him after he had tricked her into hating Matt?

Spencer hung up and sat on the bench. Or at least that's how it sounded to Ashley.

She turned her head to watch for Matt. After what felt like two hours, she had finally seen a speck of light coming from the same direction as Spencer before. The light from the flashlight traveled from left to right, as if the person who had been carrying it was afraid of something. Ashley wouldn't be surprised if Matt was acting frightened on purpose.

A few minutes later, she saw the light traveling across the bench. It was put out the instant it pointed at Spencer. Ashley clicked the record button on the voice recorder and made sure the small red dot was flashing.

"Hello, my dear friend," Spencer said. There had been so much arrogance in his voice that she wanted to punch him in the face. "Business first. Hands up."

"Why?" Matt said.

"Hands up. I don't want you playing any tricks on me."

Spencer patted him down. "Okay, now we can talk."

"Who you are? And what do you want from me?" Matt's tone was perfect. It had a hint of fear mixed with confusion, but not too much to make you wonder if he was pretending.

"What about your manners? Why don't you introduce yourself first?"

"I'm Matt Hansen. And I believe you're Spencer Cross."

"That's correct."

"Now, what do you want from me?"

Ashley couldn't resist a smile. It had been Spencer who was blackmailing poor frightened Matt, but it seemed the other way around with Matt asking questions.

"I want you to leave town."

"Leave town? What for?"

"Just pack your stuff and leave."

"Or?"

"Or we'll go through with our friendly promise to your buddies back at the shelter and make their life a pain in the ass."

"We?"

"None of your business who. You have three days to leave. If you leave, we'll call them, apologize for the inconvenience and everything will go back to normal."

"Why do you want me to leave? What do you have to gain?"

"You will leave Ashley alone."

"Ashley Madison?"

"Is there any other Ashley you've been banging the last few weeks?"

Ashley felt her cheeks flushing with blood. She was tempted to leave her hiding place and strangle Spencer right there.

"We're no longer together."

"As long as you're here, there will be a risk she'll get back with you."

"Why is it even your business? You're her ex-boyfriend."

"Ex-boyfriend or not, I won't let her hang out with a rich prick. Besides, who is going to comfort her when you're gone?"

"Do you seriously think she'll get back with you?"

"Okay, pretty boy, enough. You have three days to pack your things. If you don't, the shelter is gone." Ashley heard excitement in his voice, as if it was the most ingenious plan ever. "Ashley would be heartbroken. And she would blame you. If you leave, at least she would think you were decent enough to change your plans."

"But…"

"Shut up. Three days."

Spencer turned on his flashlight. He pointed it on the narrow trail ahead and sauntered off.

Ashley sat in silence for another few minutes to make sure Spencer wouldn't return. She followed the light from his flashlight up to the moment it disappeared in what seemed like the edge of the forest.

"Can I come out now?" she whispered.

"I think he's gone."

Ashley rose from her hiding place and stumbled to Matt. Her legs were cramped after sitting in the same position for so long. At least she got used to the darkness and could see Matt's face well enough to give him a kiss in the lips.

"Did you record it?" he asked.

"Right from the moment he opened his mouth."

"My girl."

Matt pulled her into his arms. Ashley trembled. She had been sitting in the same place for almost two hours. Her light sweater hadn't been enough to keep her warm after the sun went over the horizon.

"Are you cold?"

"Just a little."

"Here, take my sweater." Matt took off his navy wool sweater and handed it to her. She put it on herself. It smelled of oranges and reminded her of their first kiss at the top of the hill.

"Let's go. He's long gone by now."

Matt took Ashley's hand in his and turned on his flashlight. They walked together back to the town in silence.

***

"What's our next move?" Ashley asked.

They sat on a sofa in Ashley's living room. Matt threw Violet a light green squeaky ball. She ran after the toy, her tail wagging like a propeller.

"Let's make some copies of the conversation. Then we confront him tomorrow."

"When do we speak with James and Melinda?"

"After we take care of Spencer."

Take care of Spencer. Ashley imagined kicking him in the balls and throwing him out of town in his stinking old Acura. If she couldn't do the former, the latter would work, too.

"What about his lawyer?"

Violet came back with her toy and put it on Matt's lap. Matt threw the ball into the hallway. It bounced off the wall and into the kitchen. Violet stormed off to chase it.

Ashley realized Violet had trusted Matt the whole time. She could learn a lesson or two from her dog.

"We will make damn sure he will hear from Spencer. From what you told me about their phone conversation, the guy had been pretty nervous about it."

"Spencer had to be behind all of this. I doubt the lawyer would really sue them."

"I don't believe it, either. But Spencer needs to be taught a lesson."

"I'll call him tomorrow. I'll sob. I'll tell him you're leaving and ask him to comfort me."

"And then he'll come here, and I'll be sitting right here on this couch."

"Perfect. I can't wait to see his face."

Ashley would savor this moment of victory over her lying ex-boyfriend. She would taste it like the finest coffee, sip by sip.

Chapter 14

"He's coming," Ashley said.

She stood at the kitchen window and watched Spencer get out of his car. He wore a white dress shirt and gray slacks. Dressed up as if he had a reason to celebrate. Ashley would make damn sure he would have a reason to celebrate. Celebrate that he wouldn't go to prison.

"Sofa it is," Matt said.

He rose up from the chair and went to the living room. Violet followed him with a wagging tail, ready to play with the ball. Last night, they moved the sofa deeper into the room so that Spencer wouldn't see Matt sitting in the room before he entered it. They didn't want to risk him getting away before listening to the recording of the conversation.

Ashley put aside the onions she had cut to make her look as if she was crying. She smeared her make-up and trotted over to the front door. The doorbell rang.

She exhaled a long breath. It was time to roll.

"Oh, Spencer, how good to see you," she said in a sad voice with a hint of happiness.

"Hey Ashley. Are you all right?"

She would be in just a minute.

"I… I'm so… Matt called. He told me he's leaving town. He lied to me about everything." She broke into a sob and put her hands on his shoulders. Oh, how much she hated touching him. But it would make for even more satisfaction when she would see the look on his face in about thirty seconds.

"It's okay, babe. It's okay." Spencer took her into an embrace. His hand stroked her back. Ashley was sure he had a smirk on his face. It would be wiped off in about twenty seconds.

"Let's go to the living room. I will tell you everything." She broke the embrace and almost exhaled a breath of relief. It disgusted her to even touch him.

She motioned Spencer to go first. He walked down the corridor and turned right. Ashley walked right behind him.

"So–" His head turned right and he saw Matt sitting on the sofa with Violet sitting right beside him. They both stared at him with grim expressions on their faces.

Ashley couldn't help it. She burst out laughing. Spencer's eyes were wide in shock, his mouth agape, and all the color drained from his face. His entire body was frozen up. He reminded her of a caveman in a block of ice, seconds after he saw ice cracking under his legs.

Ashley closed the door behind her with a thud and leaned on it. Spencer turned around in shock. The cold fear in his eyes made her howl with laughter. The look on his face was priceless. It was the closest thing that could repay all his lies, and all the pain he had inflicted on her.

"What the hell are you doing?"

"Teaching you a lesson. Sit down." Matt pointed to a white chair she had brought from the kitchen. The grave look on Matt's face made Ashley stop laughing. She didn't want him to beat Spencer.

"What are you doing here? I told you what would happen if you didn't leave," Spencer said in a shaky voice.

"Sit down, I said."

Spencer plodded to the chair.

"Do you recognize it?" Matt played the recording of their conversation the day before. Spencer's mouth once again went agape. His hands trembled.

"What is that?"

"It's the proof you blackmailed me. Ready to send to the authorities."

"You wouldn't do it."

"Why not? We have real evidence against you. What do you have against us?"

Spencer's eyes moved from left to right. He wriggled on his chair. He looked as if he would have a heart attack.

"I…"

"You, my dear friend, will call your partner right now. You will tell him that if he doesn't want to go to prison, he is to call the shelter right away and tell them it was just a misunderstanding."

"I—"

"Stop talking, start dialing." Matt pointed to Spencer's pocket. Ashley was surprised to see him in so much control over the situation. She guessed being a CEO had made him a tough negotiator.

Spencer pulled out his phone and dialed someone.

"Pete? I… there's a situation." He glanced at Matt with fear. "You need to call the shelter right now and tell them it was all a misunderstanding."

The room fell silent. Ashley heard some muffled sounds from the speaker.

"Shut up and listen to me. Call them right now if you don't want to go to prison." Spencer hung up.

"Now we wait," Matt said.

They sat in silence for a few uncomfortable minutes. Spencer sat on the chair with his head bowed down.

Ashley's cell phone broke the silence. It was Melinda.

"Ashley? Ashley, the lawyer called us again. He apologized and told us it was a misunderstanding. We can keep the money and there will be no lawsuit," Melinda said everything so quickly that Ashley barely made out the words.

"Oh my God. I'm so happy to hear that, Melinda. It's such great news."

Melinda babbled in a cheery voice for another minute or two.

"Yes, Melinda, I will be at the shelter tomorrow. We will definitely have to celebrate it."

She hung up and stared at Spencer, who exhaled a long breath.

"Can I go now?" he asked.

"You can go and pack your things," Matt said.

"Do what?"

"I've told you. If you're still here three days from now, a CD with this recording will go to the press. Police next."

"I—"

"You're in no position to bargain with me. Three days, or you'll go to prison." Matt's commanding voice reminded Ashley of the way drill sergeants spoke to their soldiers.

"Now get the hell out," Matt said.

Spencer rose up from his chair, stole a glance at Ashley and left the house in a hurry.

"Now what? The shelter?" Matt said in a gentle voice.

"Let them celebrate together. We can explain everything later."

"Let's go on a walk then."

"With Violet and Duke."

"Sure thing, honey."

Matt took her hand in his. Their fingers interlocked. They left Ashley's home with Violet trotting right beside them.

Fifteen minutes later, they crossed the street where they had met for the first time. Duke and Violet chased after each other like two great friends. Matt held Ashley's hand in a gentle grip. Ashley turned her head and gazed into his eyes.

"You know what? I'm actually happy you almost ran us over a few weeks ago."

How You Can Help

Did you enjoy this book? Want to help spread the word? Please consider leaving a review.

Reviews and word-of-mouth help other readers discover my work. As an independent author, I don't have a huge promotional budget. Your review, even if it's just a paragraph or two, would be of immense help.

Thank you,

Ava

Get Updates

Would you like to get updates about new books? If so, sign up for my mailing list by visiting the link below:

http://www.bsmpublishing.com/ava

Books by Ava Summers

Lucky Dog Series

Love Me, Love My Dog

Forty-three-year old Samantha Anderson is a romance novel writer who has recently moved to a small town of Maple Hills to escape the bad memories of her divorce. There, she finds a friend in an intelligent Irish Wolfhound.

When her dog gets ill, she takes him to a local veterinarian, who turns out to be a good-natured and handsome thirty-something man. What role will her dog play in making them cross her path with the vet again? Would Samantha be able to open her heart after being left by her husband for a much younger woman?

Every Dog Has Its Day

Thirty-five-year-old Laura Rogers is a freelance writer who has been living as a single woman her entire life in a small town of Maple Hills. Her best friend is a Bernese Mountain Dog named Lucky.

When her dog disappears, Laura's life turns upside down – until the moment the muscular thirty-something personal trainer Richard Tanner finds Lucky wounded in the woods and reunites the dog with Laura. Would she be able to break her lifelong habits and let Richard stay in her life for longer than a brief moment?

A Dog's Life

Thirty-four-year-old Ashley Madison is a freelance web designer working part time at the local Italian restaurant. After breaking up with her unfaithful boyfriend Spencer, she lives a dull and unsatisfying life. She shares it with her female Irish Setter Violet and animals from the local animal shelter where Ashley volunteers.

Ashley's life is turned upside down when her dog is almost ran over by Matt Hansen, a thirty-seven-year-old retired wealthy businessman who has just moved to the small town of Maple Hills.

Will Ashley be able to overcome her distrust of men, call off the dogs and let Matt enter her life?

Printed in Great Britain
by Amazon